Cecilia Valetti was born and raised in Italy. She has been an English language and literature teacher for almost three decades. She lives in a village in the north of Italy with her husband.

A New Beginning:
Miracle High School Mysteries

Cecilia Valetti

A New Beginning:
Miracle High School Mysteries

Vanguard Press

VANGUARD PAPERBACK

© Copyright 2024
Cecilia Valetti

The right of Cecilia Valetti to be identified as author of
this work has been asserted by her in accordance with the
Copyright, Designs and Patents Act 1988.

All Rights Reserved

No reproduction, copy or transmission of this publication
may be made without written permission.
No paragraph of this publication may be reproduced,
copied or transmitted save with the written permission of the
publisher, or in accordance with the provisions
of the Copyright Act 1956 (as amended).

Any person who commits any unauthorised act in relation to
this publication may be liable to criminal
prosecution and civil claims for damages.

A CIP catalogue record for this title is
available from the British Library.

ISBN 978 1 80016 988 3

This is a work of fiction. Names, characters, businesses, places, events and
incidents are either the product of the author's imagination or used in a
fictitious manner. Any resemblance to actual persons, living or dead, or actual
events is purely coincidental.

Vanguard Press is an imprint of
Pegasus Elliot Mackenzie Publishers Ltd.
www.pegasuspublishers.com

First Published in 2024

Vanguard Press
Sheraton House Castle Park
Cambridge England

Printed & Bound in Great Britain

This novel is dedicated to my dear late father, who inspired the figure of Maria's dad, and to my darling husband, who has made my life wonderful

Prologue

Trinity, Ontario, Thursday, September 18th

After a few minutes, he heard footsteps in the deserted corridor and he called out,

"I am here in our office." He thought, 'What will he say when he discovers that I have invented an excuse to be sure he will show up at a time when he doesn't like to leave his home? What will he say when I tell him what I have done and what they have ordered me to do?'

He turned to face the door of the office and he saw a dark silhouette in the doorway. He didn't have time to think of what was happening. He certainly didn't expect THIS thing to happen and he stared blankly at the shining blade that was going to hit him... Just a moment and then... a pain in his chest, blood... and... darkness!

Chapter 1

Flight Venice-Toronto, Wednesday, August 27th

Looking out of the porthole, Maria was gazing at the amazing scenery below the plane: the wonderful mountain landscape of the Alps. She had never left Italy, her home country, in her life, and this time she was not leaving for a short holiday, she was beginning a new experience in a country she had often dreamt of but she had never seen; Canada. This was the opportunity she had longed for since she had become an Italian language teacher almost thirteen years before and when Father Giulio had called her to tell her about this possibility of teaching abroad, at first she had thought it was only a dream… But Father Giulio had something more to tell her, something more difficult to hear and accept… He had given her the letter she was now holding in her hand. She'd read it a hundred times in the past months. The letter had been written by her father who had died six months before her departure. He had decided to write a long message to his daughter to reveal something he had never had the courage to tell her in person, a truth that was really difficult to digest, but that helped to explain many events in her past. She opened the letter with trembling hands and a lump in her throat and read once again.

"My dearest Maria, first of all, let me tell you that I sincerely hope that what I am writing will not affect the remembrance of the years we shared as father and daughter, especially after my wife died twelve years ago. I have learned to love you and to appreciate your sweetness, your trustworthiness and your sincerity even more, but... maybe, because of this harmony we had created, I didn't find the courage to tell you a truth that doesn't lessen in any way my love for you as the daughter who has given me such comfort in every moment. When your sister was eight-years-old, Father Giulio called your mum and me — he knew we would have liked to have another child, but your mum had problems during your sister's delivery and she was scared. Father Giulio told us that a very young girl (she was seventeen at that time), coming from Canada, was in Italy on a student exchange when she discovered she was pregnant. She was worried and confused, and at first, she didn't want to keep her baby, but Father Giulio convinced her to renounce the abortion, promising that, once the baby was born, she could leave her at the hospital in complete anonymity, as the law in Italy grants. Father Giulio told us that the baby was due in three months and asked if we would consider the adoption. That wonderful little baby that was born in July was YOU, my darling."

Maria had difficulty holding back the tears when she reached this point in the letter and she had to stop for a few moments. On one side, she thanked God that she had been adopted by her family and had been spared living in a foster home or an orphanage, but on the other side, she understood only now her mum's and sister's attitudes towards her, some knowing smiles they exchanged, some harsh words they said to her... The constant hint of her not being like her sister, the veiled envy when she started to get good marks at school — better than her sister, to tell the truth! And the painful expression on her dad's face when he noticed this behaviour. She was, in fact, very different from her stepsister in everything, from the physical aspect to the personality.

Maria was slim but not very tall, she had shoulder-length light brown, wavy hair, a small nose and green eyes, which nobody in her family had. Her sister was tall like her dad but she was not very slim, she had dark eyes and dark, straight hair. Maria was very sweet, sensitive and generally cheerful, while her sister was pessimistic and often in a bad mood. Maria didn't like elegant clothes, she dressed casually, she liked wearing blue jeans and a T-shirt or a sweater, her sister liked dresses, high-heeled shoes and expensive bags.

Maria resumed her father's letter.

"I was very happy to have you in our family, to give a sister to my child, I imagined you growing up together. Your mum, instead, was not easy to convince, she kept saying

that she would never be able to consider you and your sister as her two children, and in fact, she was never able to treat you as her child — I know that and this was a cause of great distress and suffering for me, and I know, for you too. Instead of growing fond of you and of teaching your sister to love you, your mum became more and more distant and hostile as the years went by. You can't imagine how many times I begged her to change her attitude but she never listened to me. Then, when you were at university, I implored her to tell you the truth but she never agreed, in fact, she forbade me to talk to you about your adoption... After her death, I tried to find a justification for her behaviour, but in all these years, I have not been able to find any and it surely is not your fault because you were always kind and considerate to her and you assisted her with great affection at the time of her illness."

Maria was reliving all the harshness of her mum and sister and a great bitterness pervaded her...

"You will certainly ask questions about your real mom, but I must tell you that we never knew her name and that Father Giulio had recently told me he has lost all trace of her since she went back to her family immediately after your birth.

My darling, I hope you will forgive me for not telling you the truth in person... If only your mum had agreed for us to speak to you together! What I can tell you is that I love you with all my heart and I have always been grateful to the Divine Providence for having adopted you, because you have brought affection into my existence... I hope God will help you to accept my weakness and that you'll never doubt my love.

Your Dad"

Maria folded the letter and placed it once more in the envelope, thinking of her dad with great affection and longing. When her sister, Raffaella, was in her early twenties, she had gone to live in Bologna where she had had one boyfriend after the other but she had never introduced them to her family. She had kept at a distance until her mum had become ill, and after a few months, had died, twelve years before. In those months, she had sometimes come home to visit her. After her stepmother's death, Maria remained with her dad and they had seen her sister just a few times, even in the last months of her dad's life.

She couldn't help considering these years a time of grace, because Maria and her dad had shared many pleasant and peaceful moments, especially in the evenings when they sat in her dad's study to read or to discuss the events of the day, or at the weekends when they went together to visit a neighbouring town or a museum. They had really developed a deep understanding, and even if Maria kept wondering why her dad had not found the right time to tell her about her adoption in person, she had already forgiven him in her heart, because of the precious years together she would always cherish. She had more difficulties forgetting and forgiving her stepmother and stepsister because their attitude hurt her more now than in the past. Why had her mother always refused to tell her she had been adopted if it was obvious she didn't love her? The answer that came to Maria's mind was because her mum found pleasure in teasing and tormenting her. This was a terrible answer but it was the only one that she could find.

These were more or less the things Father Giulio had told her when she had gone to him the day after reading the letter for the first time, full of questions and doubts and longing for comfort and support from the man who had known her father better than anyone else.

When Maria entered Father Giulio's parlour, she was full of anger and resentment towards her dad for not having told her the truth while he was alive, but she was disappointed in Father Giulio as well because he had not convinced her father to talk to her. The priest welcomed her with a sad expression on his face, full of sympathy for what she was going through after reading her dad's letter.

"Come and sit down, Maria, and don't be too fast in judging your father's behaviour."

Maria, looking at the old minister, had felt her frustration begin to subside. In her heart, she knew that the two people who loved her most had certainly done what they thought was better for her, but oh, how difficult it was to accept this. She had sat down on the armchair in front of the big desk.

"Oh, Giulio! Why didn't my dad tell me? I would have certainly understood! I feel hurt, betrayed and I am wondering whether he didn't tell me only because he was afraid of losing me and remaining alone."

"Oh, no, Maria!" The priest had put a soothing hand on her shoulder, "he never doubted your affection for him, but telling you that you had been adopted as a baby made him feel guilty for not being able to convince your mum and your sister to accept and love you. You know, when I called him and your mom to tell them that I had convinced a young girl to give birth to her baby, your dad immediately offered to adopt you but he had a hard time convincing your mother. Then he was always aware that your mum never really accepted you and it was painful for him to see that your mother seemed to enjoy treating you in such a harsh way, and at the same time, refusing to tell you the truth. But Maria," Father Giulio had sat down on a chair next to her and taken her hand in his, "I can assure you, your dad did everything he could to change the situation and he always loved you, even more in these last years that he considered a blessing."

Maria had felt tears rolling down her cheeks, and for a few minutes, she had been unable to speak, she had just let the silent presence of Father Giulio soothe her.

Finally, she had regained her composure. "Giulio, I knew that talking to you would do me good, but now I need some time to sort everything out. I don't know if I still want to go to teach abroad, I am so sad and I feel so lonely…"

"You don't have to take any decisions now that you are so upset, Maria, but don't abandon your dream of teaching Italian abroad now that you finally have this opportunity. Furthermore," he had added with a smile, "Canada is YOUR country a little, don't you think?"

"Do you know anything about my real mum, now she should be in her fifties. Where does she live? Maybe I will be able to meet her if I go to Canada to teach, even if now I don't know if I would like to see her after so many years…" Maria's voice reflected the agitation she was experiencing.

Father Giulio had smiled and then answered, choosing his words carefully, " Your mum and dad never met or even saw the girl, I don't remember her name and the Italian law protects the anonymity of the mother because she was underage at that time. I think she came from Toronto or Ottawa but she went back to her family as soon as it was possible after your birth and I have never heard from her. Your natural father was a young Italian boy, whose family immediately convinced him not to recognize you as his daughter. So your real mum went through the pregnancy alone, supported only by our community. She was a very courageous girl and I know she suffered when she had to leave you, but she has never kept in touch with us, maybe it was too painful for her. If she had asked to meet you, we could have revealed her name to you, but she has never tried to find you, so, even if I remembered her name, I couldn't tell you."

When Maria left the priest, she felt a little better but still confused. Of all the countries in the world, she had always felt attracted to Canada. Was it a sign that she had a connection with this country? Was it just a coincidence that she was being offered a job there, or was her father guiding her to discover something about her past? She had always believed that the people we love in our lives continue to follow us after their death and she had often dreamt of her dad since he had left her; in her dreams, he was always smiling and he seemed happy and this was a great comfort to her, she felt so lonely without his presence…

After a few days, she had called Father Giulio to tell him she intended to accept the offer she had received from Miracle High School in the town of Trinity, and the priest had put her in touch with Father Mark, the director of the school. They had exchanged emails and talked on the phone a few times and she had started to like the Canadian clergyman — he was very affable and kind, he immediately offered his condolences for the death of Maria's father and said he was looking forward to meeting her in person. He even offered to find her a little home to rent. Maria decided she would not look for her natural mum, since she had not tried to get in touch with her daughter in thirty-seven years. She didn't bear a grudge against her, but she just wanted to concentrate on her new life, on this new exciting experience that was awaiting her. When she had talked to Father Giulio a few days before her flight to Toronto, he had approved of her decision, saying it would be really difficult to find a person she knew so little about and that this research would be for her only a source of grief in such an important moment in her life.

***

Maria looked through the photos she had saved on her tablet — Father Mark had sent her some pictures of the little home he had selected for her. It was a little one-storey bungalow on the outskirts of the town with a small garden in front. It looked very cosy and comfortable.

Maria would have liked to keep her father's home a little longer because she wanted a place to be able to go back to in case she didn't like her job in Canada or her contract would not be renewed after the school year, but she had had to sell it before leaving because her stepsister Raffaella wanted to split the money — this was the last time she had seen her, in front of the notary. When they had met in front of the family notary for the Succession Act, her sister had not spared her some harsh and tactless remarks. She relived that moment with sadness and bitterness. Raffaella didn't know about her father's letter to Maria and maybe she thought her sister still didn't know about the adoption. When they were ready to sign the papers for the inheritance, she had said sarcastically, "I think you must know that you are not my sister, because you were adopted at birth. I really don't think you should have your share of inheritance after all the support you have received from my family." Maria had not answered and Raffaella had been surprised because she had expected a shocked reaction on Maria's part, but the notary, who was an old friend of her father's and knew about the letter, had stopped her immediately, and said, "Miss Raffaella, I think you should stop before saying something even nastier because Miss Maria knows everything about her adoption, and you know, as everyone in Italy knows, that an adopted child has the same rights as a natural child, and…" here he had paused and looked at the troubled face of Maria with sadness and sympathy, "your father recently told me that he had not seen you, Raffaella, or heard from you for a very long time, even if you knew he was not well, and how saddened he was by your behaviour." Raffaella had not said a word, she had signed the papers and left, without even saying goodbye.

Now Maria felt completely alone, facing a new life with no connection to her past since even the house she had shared with her father had been sold. If she decided or she had to go back to Italy after the one-year contract, she would have to find a new home for herself… But now she didn't want to think about it… The only things she had kept of her dear father's were the photos of their trips together and his wedding ring, which was really precious to her and she kept on a gold chain around her neck. He had given it to her a few days before his death, accompanying the gift with words that still rang in Maria's ears, "Maria, this is my wedding ring, that is the most precious thing I have. I would like you to keep it and to give it to your future husband because I am sure you will find a wonderful man who will love you with all his heart…" Touching it now, she felt her father beside her, smiling and encouraging her as he had always done.

She looked through some photos of the town she would live in, Trinity. She had found them on the internet. It was a beautiful little town on the shore of Lake Ontario, north of Toronto, with a lot of green places and she had already noticed some pleasant paths where she could walk and relax. In her free time, she had always liked to take walks in parks or hike in the mountains. Trinity looked so different from her hometown, Padua, in the north of Italy. Padua was not a big town, but as every town in Italy, it was historical with many ancient monuments, while Trinity seemed more modern, but very well kept, tidy and clean. It resembled more small towns or villages in Italy, with a main street lined with little shops, a square with a statue in the middle and the town hall, and a little park with swings and slides for children. A beautiful church in the centre of the town with a tall steeple was similar to churches in small villages in the north of Italy and the school she would teach at was in the immediate suburbs, not far from "her" bungalow. She really liked this town and she was looking forward to getting to know more about the Canadian way of living.

***

After a pleasant, uneventful flight, finally, the plane began its descent towards the airport of Toronto. The only metropolis Maria had seen in her life was Milan, the biggest town in Italy with more than one million inhabitants. She preferred living in a smaller town but it was fascinating to see the skyline, with many tall buildings but also green parks, the lake and the outskirts with little houses. She knew that many Italian people lived in Canada, because the period between the two World Wars and after the Second World War had been very hard for many Italian families, who had to emigrate in order to find better jobs and to be able to give a more serene life to their children, who were now Canadian citizens. She was looking forward to visiting Toronto, to seeing the view from the CN Tower, walking along the streets, doing some shopping, visiting the museums... How many new things were awaiting her, how many new experiences, new acquaintances... This new beginning had a great appeal for her, but at the same time, it frightened her because, even if she had always been a good teacher loved by colleagues and students, she kept wondering if she would be able to do a good job here, with students from a completely different background, with different habits, a different mentality and outlook. She hoped she would always find a way to conquer the hearts and the trust of her young students, because she liked to talk to them and to listen to their stories, to be able to guide them in their choices.

As the plane was landing, Maria closed her eyes, "Dear Dad, please help and assist me in this new life I am beginning and guide me as you have always done with your love!" During the last six months, she had started to talk to her dad whenever she was sad or when she needed support. This made her feel immediately better and at peace. She constantly felt his presence and she confided in his unending affection and protection. Now she was ready for A NEW BEGINNING.

Chapter 2

Trinity, Thursday, August 28th

Maria woke up early the following day. She got up and looked around her little bungalow. While she was still in Italy, Father Mark had found a little home for rent for her and he had told her this little one-floor house was not far from the school, so that, at least at first, she wouldn't be obliged to have a car. The bungalow was ten minutes on foot from Miracle High School and a pleasant twenty to twenty-five minute walk from the High Street and the centre of the town. Not far from the house, there was also a small shopping mall with a supermarket. Maria didn't mind walking, in fact, she liked it, and in her hometown, she used her car only to go shopping or to visit another town. In Padua, she always walked or took the bus.

Father Mark had told her that the secretary of the school, Mrs Angela Dawson, had done some basic food shopping for her and had taken care of all the things she could need in the first few days. She had been really kind and Maria was thinking of a little present for her to express her gratitude.

Maria had arrived the previous day in the late afternoon from the airport and she was really tired because of the long journey and the jet lag. So, after unpacking, she had gone to bed early and now she felt refreshed and ready to discover this new place.

First of all, she looked around. Her new home was really small, her bedroom was large enough to contain a double bed, a wardrobe and a chest of drawers. In a corner of the wardrobe, she found some blankets, bed linen and towels. Next to the bedroom, there was a fairly large bathroom, with a tub and a shower. In a corner of the bathroom, there was also a top-loading washing machine. A small corridor led to the living-dining room, with a sofa bed and two armchairs, a fairly large table with six chairs around it and a fitted kitchen wall, with many wooden cabinets and cupboards. The kitchen furniture was similar to the one she had in Italy; light brown with brass knobs, the cooker, the oven and a double basin sink. There was a little dishwasher under the sink. In the cupboards and the cabinets, there were just some plates, cups, saucers, cutlery and utensils, so Maria decided to make a note in the following days of the things she may need. From Italy, she had brought her moka pot, in reality, one small moka for herself and one for three cups in case she had guests. In a corner of the worktop, she saw an electric kettle she could use to prepare tea or a tisane. She had gotten used to drinking herbal tea after dinner with her dad, and after he had died, she had continued to do so even if every time memories of so many happy moments came to her mind and filled her heart with emotion.

In a corner of the living room under the window, there was a desk with a chair behind it. The perfect spot to correct homework and prepare lessons, she thought. There was enough space for her laptop and there were two shelves above the desk where she could keep her books, even if she had recently converted to electronic books saved in an application on her tablet. Maybe they did not entirely substitute for traditional ones but helped to save a lot of space.

A little foyer led to the front door. She opened it and saw that just three steps separated the house from a little but pleasant garden. In Italy, she lived in a block of flats in a residential area but she had always missed a garden or a green space, especially in the last months of her dad's life when he would have enjoyed sitting outside. In the garden, there was a short path that led to the street and this struck Maria because there was no fence. In Italy this would have been impossible, every garden was separated from the others and the street by high hedges or iron or wooden fences. The only difference between her home and the one next to hers was the fact that she did not have a garage. It was not a problem for her now because she didn't intend to have a car soon.

She went back into the house and walked to the back door in the kitchen. There was a tiny backyard. This had a fence behind it and she reflected that, even if it was really small, it would be pleasant to sit on a chair or on a bench to read in the evening or just to relax.

Maria had noticed during her tour of the house that there were some sticky notes on the desk, together with a map of the town of Trinity and a coach timetable. Now, she took the laptop from her bag, sat down on the chair and read the notes. One was a list of phone numbers: Father Mark's, Mrs Dawson's and the school office. On another one, there were the first important school meetings for the following days with dates and times. The third note was written by Mrs Dawson, "Welcome to Canada, if you need anything, call me! Angela."

Maria decided to call her immediately to thank her for her kindness. She took her mobile phone. At the airport, she bought a Canadian SIM card and she had substituted it for the Italian one. She thought sadly that she had no one in Italy to tell that she was all right, apart from Father Giulio… No family, no connections to her home country, just a few friends and colleagues.

Mrs Dawson answered after a few rings.

"Mrs Dawson, it's Maria Busati. I arrived from Italy yesterday!"

"Miss Busati, welcome to Canada and to our town. I hope you will feel at home here!" The enthusiastic and very kind voice certainly made her feel at home. "And please, call me Angela. Everybody at school uses first names!"

"Thanks, Angela, and I am Maria. I am very glad to be here, I was looking forward to my new experience…

Thanks for doing the shopping for me and for everything I have found in my new home." Maria looked at the school calendar on her desk and added, " I think I will see you tomorrow!"

"Yes," Mrs Dawson replied, "we are all looking forward to meeting you, and you'll see, Father Mark has been wonderful in the last few years at creating the atmosphere of a real family in our staff. We like working together and also our students perceive this spirit of cooperation and this harmony that there is among us." Maria felt the affection of the secretary for the people who worked at and attended her school and for Father Mark.

"Thanks, Angela, I hope I will be able to give my contribution. I have always liked teaching and working with teenagers. See you tomorrow, then, and thanks again."

"See you, Maria…" Maria ended the call feeling a little less lonely and abandoned. She was in a foreign country, and behind her, in her home country, she felt a great void, but in front of her, she expected a world full of new acquaintances, new friends, new experiences… She was really eager to start.

***

Steve was looking forward to finishing work at the Kilton Motor Company because he would drive to Oshawa to meet his new girlfriend. This time he felt she was the right one. She was not like his previous girlfriends or lovers. Jill was a good girl; she had her regular job at the hairdresser's salon near her home, she liked a quiet life, going to the cinema, going for a walk, going shopping, not expensive parties or dangerous hobbies like Steve's. In fact, he had not dared to tell her about his habits, about that diner, the Trucker, where he spent his Friday and Saturday nights playing cards and spending money with disreputable 'friends'. She only knew he worked as an accountant in a car dealing company in Trinity and that he lived alone outside the town. He had met her in Trinity a few months before when she had come to his town to visit a friend. They were walking on the path along the lake, chatting and laughing, and he was taking a walk after work. One of the girls had inadvertently dropped her mobile phone, he had picked it up and given it back to her. They started chatting, and in the end, they exchanged mobile phone numbers. After a few days, he had called her, and from that moment, they had started meeting occasionally, mainly to go to the cinema, they had once gone to Toronto to watch a baseball game.

As soon as he left the office, he took his car and drove to Oshawa, it was just more or less half an hour by car. He arrived just when Jill and her colleagues were closing the salon. Jill smiled at him and invited him to her home for a cup of coffee before going to eat out together. They usually went to a little diner in the centre of Oshawa; very intimate and cosy and not too expensive.

Steve was not a handsome man, but he had a pleasant smile, was tall and slim, in his late thirties but he looked younger, maybe because he had a perennial boyish face. Jill, instead, looked older than her age, perhaps because of the heavy make-up she constantly applied to her face, but she had a sweet smile.

While she was getting ready to go out and he was sitting in her living room, his phone rang. He looked at the caller ID and his expression became visibly worried,

"Hi," he said curtly, while Jill was coming back into the living room. Steve listened for a few minutes and then tried to sound calm when he said, "OK, but I had told you not to call me tonight. See you tomorrow at the usual place and time." On the other end, the voice kept on talking and Steve looked really nervous. "Can't we talk tomorrow? I see no reason for discussing this now. I will be there, OK?" And he ended the call without waiting for an answer. It was not the first time Jill had witnessed a similar call, but when she had asked him what the matter was, the answers had been evasive and vague: problems at work, a discussion with a friend...

She looked at him now and commented ironically, "You seem to have a lot of discussions with your friends!"

Steve looked at her imploringly, "Please, Jill, stay out of it!"

But during the dinner, Jill said in a serious tone, "Steve, I know you are worried about something and you are often distracted, you keep looking at that mobile phone as if it could explode. I like being with you, I think you are a good man and you are always kind and considerate. I have seldom found such a gentle and pleasant man as you, but I think you have a kind of second life, a life that I know nothing about and where you don't want me, a life that I feel I wouldn't like. If you have a problem we can face it together. I don't want secrets between us, at least if your intentions are serious. I have no secrets for you. Please, Steve," she had added, looking at him with affection.

Steve took her hand in his and told her, "Please, Jill, if I ask you to stay out of it, I really mean it. I have big, big problems with some guys I don't want you to even meet…" his voice trailed off and Jill decided not to press him to explain. She was really feeling something for this man who was completely different from the men she had gone out with before. She was used to demanding men, who always thought more about her beauty and attractiveness and less about her feelings. Steve was always kind, he cared about her feelings, he was very attentive to her words, to her opinions.

The rest of the evening was spent talking about their colleagues, their work and she didn't press him further but she silently made up her mind to try to find out something more about this dark side of his life.

***

Maria spent her first day in Canada in a pleasant and quiet way. She went to do some shopping in the nearby shopping mall and then she explored the path that bordered the lake. It was really a pleasant walk among the trees and the flowers in the luxuriant late summer nature. When the path reached the centre of the town, there was a small harbour and a pedestrian walk that led to a little lighthouse. She decided not to explore it that evening, but she felt that this would become one of her favourite places, so peaceful and pleasant. At sunset, Maria stopped on a bench and watched the beauty of the colours of the sun on the lake. She thought of her life so far, full of satisfaction in her job but so devoid of love in her family; only her dad had given her affection and a real sense of family life. Her stepmother and stepsister had done their best to make her feel outside their family, even if she didn't know at that time that she did not belong to it. She reflected that her dad had not become her stepfather in her heart after reading his letter, while she had instinctively detached herself from her sister and mother whom she now referred to as stepmother and - sister.

She sighed and stood up, it was getting cooler now that the sun had set and she decided to go back home and make dinner.

Before going out she had written an email to Father Giulio, the only person in Italy who had asked her to keep in touch.

'Dear Giulio, here I am in Canada. I still can't believe that my dream of teaching Italian abroad is finally coming true and that my wish to visit Canada is being fulfilled.

I arrived yesterday after a pleasant flight at the airport in Toronto. It was wonderful to see the skyline from above as we were approaching the city. It must be a wonderful town and I am looking forward to visiting it. Father Mark was at the airport and he drove me to Trinity, where I am going to live. I can understand now all the things you told me about Mark, he is really a joyful man and it is comforting and pleasant to hear him talk. He has a positive vision of life and I think he has a great heart and an enormous faith in God's Providence. I believe I have a lot to learn from him. He has been living in the Community of Miracle High School here in Trinity for five years now, before that, he used to live in Toronto. From the way he talks, you can immediately understand that he loves his students and his staff and he considers the school as a family.

We took a highway that first passed through the city of Toronto but then went along the lake with beautiful landscapes, small towns or villages. It gave me an impression of great peace and serenity, but just a few miles from a big metropolis like Toronto. Giulio, I must tell you: no soccer stadiums here but diamond-shaped baseball fields. Father Mark told me that they practice baseball and basketball at school, I am looking forward to getting to know baseball, which is totally new for me.

I have already seen beautiful paths along the lake where I can walk when I have time, you know how much I love walking.

Father Mark has found a beautiful bungalow for me, it is near the school and not far from the centre of the town, there is also a small shopping mall nearby. I enclose some photos of my new home and the garden for you to see.

Tomorrow I am visiting the school for the first time, even if I have already seen it from outside. I will have a meeting with my new colleagues and the staff, and next Tuesday, school will start. Monday is Labour day, a kind of 'Festa dei Lavoratori' in Italy. I am so excited, Giulio. Will I be able to teach in a completely different surrounding, will I be a good teacher for these students who have a different background, a different mentality? And the families? Will I be able to approach parents in the right way? Oh, Giulio, I have so many questions... But I am following your advice, I am praying and I believe my dad is near me all the time. He knew how much I longed for this experience and he will support me, I am sure!

Oh, I almost forgot to tell you that I have already got in touch with a member of the staff. Mrs Angela Dawson, the secretary of the school, was asked by Father Mark to do some shopping for me and she prepared my home for my arrival. I called her to thank her and she sounded very kind and welcoming.

Giulio, I hope I have not bored you with this long email, but you know that you are the only person in Italy I care for now. Thanks for going to the cemetery to visit my dad for me. Please, keep doing it because you know that Raffaella will forget about it very soon.

I will never thank you enough for your support and for this opportunity you have offered me. Thanks for helping me and my dad in the difficult months of his illness. I will keep in touch...

Love Maria'

After dinner, Maria opened her laptop to read Italian newspapers online. Then she had a look at her emails and she found Father Giulio's answer to her long message. The priest's reply was shorter but full of affection and encouragement.

'Dear Maria,

I am so glad you have had a pleasant flight and a serene time so far. God knows you deserve serenity and satisfaction after the months of your dad's illness, his death and all the suffering that followed. Don't worry, you have always been a good knowledgeable teacher here in Italy and you will do a wonderful job wherever you go, I am sure. Mark will certainly be a great help and comfort for you. Trust him and his advice. Keep praying, Maria, because you are not alone and keep me informed about your life and your experiences. I am looking forward to receiving news from you. You can be sure that I will always remember you in my prayers and that I will visit your dad and take care of everything at the cemetery for you. May God bless you, Maria.

Love Giulio'

A tear rolled down Maria's cheek, Father Giulio's words warmed her heart and made her feel loved. She hoped she would be able to find a community that could become a family for her. God knew how much she longed for a family.

Chapter 3

Friday, August 29th

Maria got up very early the following day. She was so excited that she really couldn't lie in bed longer, even if she generally liked to remain in bed after she had woken up for a few minutes to indulge in a peaceful moment before starting her day. She looked at the photo of her dad she had on her bedside table, the first thing she had taken out of her suitcase, and she instinctively clutched the wedding ring that hung from her neck.

'Dad, help me!' she thought, sure her father was smiling from above, happy to see her daughter fulfil her dream.

She prepared breakfast, that for her was a cup of coffee, a yogurt with a few biscuits and a fruit. She got dressed. She had not brought from Italy elegant clothes, because she didn't feel at ease when she dressed up, she didn't like high-heeled shoes and skirts and she, generally, wore jeans and a shirt or a sweater. This did not mean that she was in any way untidy-looking because her slim figure and her elegant bearing made her look attractive and smart. In her experience with teenagers, she had noticed that dressing in a simple way made her look closer to them. She didn't want to appear younger or to eliminate the right distance and respect due to her role as teacher and educator, but she wanted her students to feel free to talk to her, to trust her, perceive her as a reliable and approachable person. She didn't mind spending time after the lessons if a student asked to talk to her, she didn't mind being contacted during the summer or on her day off if someone needed her help or her advice. She considered her job as much more than simple employment, as a kind of mission, a delicate mission because she dealt with people in a difficult age, who were preparing for their adult life, sometimes with tragic or challenging family situations that weighed on their hearts and forced them to take decisions bigger than their age.

She put on a light grey cotton jacket over a blue flannel shirt and she took her bag. She was ready! She stopped before opening the door, said a quick prayer and made the sign of the cross, which for her just meant, "God, I commend to You my day and everything I will be able to accomplish!"

The sun was shining and the day was pleasantly warm. Maria walked the short distance to the school and arrived in plenty of time. She had already gone to see the school from the outside the day before, but now in plain daylight, she was able to appreciate the imposing structure. The school was a red brick building, surrounded by a schoolyard with trees, benches and paths. Students could meet here before or after lessons, talk, chat, revise what they had studied or simply walk along the paths. They could sit on the benches or the grass and stay there as long as they liked because there was no fence around the property. Next to the main entrance, there was a huge cross on the external wall that indicated that the chapel of the school was there. The chapel, which in reality was a big church, had a separate entrance because it was accessible by the parish people who went to the mass. The church was, in fact, a parish church for the Trinity Catholic community and a school chapel for Miracle High School. The main front door introduced a large hall surrounded by tall glass windows overlooking the front garden. Next to the main building, there was a lower structure for the gym, and behind it, you could see the outdoor basketball court and a baseball field with a tall net around it. In front of the school, there was a sign that directed to the car park behind it.

Maria walked up the path that led to the front entrance. A sliding glass door opened automatically in front of her and she found herself in the large hall. There was a long reception desk and a notice board beside it with various colourful notes, some handwritten and some printed.

In the hall, several small groups of two or three people were chatting cheerily. When Maria entered, Father Mark left one of these groups to approach her with a welcoming smile.

"Maria, welcome to Miracle High School." From behind the reception desk, a short plump woman with a beautiful sweet smile, green eyes and short curly blond hair came to introduce herself to her but she imagined immediately that she was the secretary she had spoken to on the phone, Mrs Dawson.

When Angela came near her, she abruptly stopped and made a strange face, as if she had seen a ghost or a person she had not met for a long time. Maria noticed that Father Mark was surprised by the secretary's reaction, also because the smile on Angela's face turned for a moment into what seemed a worried and troubled expression. But Mrs Dawson regained her composure immediately and said,

"Maria, I am so glad you are here. Come to meet your new colleagues!" The warm words made Maria forget the shocked reaction of a few instants before.

"Angela, I must thank you again for your kindness!" Maria said with equal warmth. But now Maria was surrounded by a small crowd of friendly faces and shaking hands. 'Canadian people really know how to make you feel at ease,' she thought. She turned from one face to the other and she was, for a few minutes, the centre of attention and kindness.

"Welcome to Canada!"

"I hope you had a pleasant flight!"

"Which town are you from?"

"How do you like Canada so far?"

"I love Italian cooking!"

"How long have you been teaching in Italy?"

Some remarks made her smile because they were based on common stereotypes about Italy and Italian people but everything was said to make her feel at home and she appreciated this flood of words and smiles and handshakes.

Father Mark seemed to be enjoying himself, and after a few minutes, he said, "Colleagues, let's go to the meeting room and there we can get to know Maria better."

They all went to a large room with a circular table and many swivelling chairs around it. The school looked modern in the furniture and the facilities.

In the room, there were now more or less fifteen people, only the teachers of the high school and the staff, but Maria knew that in the building there was also a middle school for younger pupils, which was in another side of the structure and there were specifically organized meetings of the two teaching bodies.

Father Mark waited until everyone had taken a seat and said, "I am so glad we are all here together at the beginning of a new school year. Before starting, let's offer a prayer for our school, our teachers, our staff members, our students and all the people we are going to meet this year. All the students who come to this school must leave it after a few years feeling they have been part of a family, they must not only know more about the subject they have chosen to study, but they must be better people, ready to face life and always aware that they can come back here whenever they need to. This is what 'school' means for me and for the Salesian order, whose mission is to take care of young boys and girls in parishes and schools. Now let's pray…" Everyone stood up and they prayed together, "Our Father" and "Hail Mary". From the countenance of the people around her, Maria could see that Father Mark was respected and loved by everyone. The priest was a short and slim man in his late sixties, with a pleasant round face and smiling light brown eyes.

After the prayers, they sat down in silence and Father Mark resumed:

"Before going into the agenda for this school year, since we have a new teacher," he smiled at Maria, "I would like each of you to introduce himself or herself. We commonly use first names here, both for colleagues and staff and for students. Please, John, break the ice!"

John stood up and said he was the Science teacher.

Then it was the turn of Julian who was the Maths teacher, Gloria was the Canadian history teacher, Melany the English literature teacher, Simon the Arts teacher, Lucas the French teacher, Dylan the computer science teacher, Greg the sports coach, Barbara the Latin teacher and Francine the Economics teacher. Maria was looking from one colleague to the other and she was trying to memorize faces and names but she thought she would need time. All the teachers were from Ontario, apart from Lucas and Simon who came from Quebec. The staff was composed of three people: the secretary Angela, the receptionist Lucinda and the accountant Robert.

Now it was Maria's turn and she was really agitated. She stood up and said, "My name is Maria, I am from

Padua in Italy." When she said the name of her hometown, Angela cast her eyes down as if she had heard something that had hurt her, but Maria didn't have time to dwell on it. "Padua is a little town in the north, not far from Venice. I graduated almost fourteen years ago in my hometown in Italian and foreign languages and I specialized in teaching techniques. I have always taught high school students in a linguistic high school and I have been teaching now for thirteen years. I have always dreamt of teaching Italian in a foreign country and I still can't believe I am fulfilling my dream now. I hope I will be able to do a good job and I think I will need your help. I thank you for your warm welcome today." She looked around at the smiling friendly faces and she felt she would really find a family here. She sat down and Father Mark started to introduce the different commitments of the year, he distributed a detailed calendar where all the holidays, the meeting days and the deadlines were indicated.

When the meeting ended, John, the Science teacher, offered immediately to take Maria on a tour of the school, so that she could familiarize herself with the different rooms and areas of the big building.

On the ground floor, apart from the reception, there were two meeting rooms of different sizes, the smallest one was used for parents' meetings. There was also a small cafeteria in a corner with some tables outside. On the first floor, there were the classrooms, Father Mark's parlour and the laboratories; one in particular, the language lab, would be useful for Maria.

John was a very pleasant guide. Maria had already noticed that all her colleagues were in their forties or early fifties, John looked a little younger, maybe late thirties. He was blond with a round face and round glasses that gave him a funny and joyful look. He was not tall and he was of medium build but he seemed an athletic man, maybe because he was wearing jeans and a light sweatshirt with the logo of the school.

After a cursory tour of the school, John led Maria to the cafeteria where some of the other colleagues were already sitting at a table. John took a chair for Maria and invited her to sit down. They all remained for an hour together, chatting and getting to know each other. Maria was really happy and enjoyed the company of these new workmates. One of her new colleagues, Julian, the Maths teacher, said, as they were leaving,

" Father Mark has told me that you have rented a bungalow not far from the school. If you need a car, my mum doesn't use her car any more because of her health problems and we would be happy to sell it to you. It is not very old and it has not been used much!"

Maria didn't need the car to go to school, but the previous day, when she had explored the town, she had thought that maybe a car could be useful if she wanted to visit nearby places. She thanked Julian and they agreed to meet one of the following days to see the car and finalize the deal.

In the early afternoon, Maria went back home, but she was invited the following Sunday to go for a walk on the lake with two or three colleagues who loved walking in nature.

When she left the school, Angela was not at the reception desk. Maria wanted to go to the office to say goodbye, but she changed her mind because there was something in the behaviour of the secretary that had upset her, even if she could not understand exactly what. Angela had reacted in a strange way to their meeting and to something Maria had said. Maybe she was just shy, maybe inadvertently Maria had said something that had hurt her. Maria thought that she would have plenty of time in the following days to talk to her or to talk to Father Mark and learn if Angela had some problems or something that worried her.

***

Jill had made up her mind. During one of Steve's unpleasant phone calls, she had heard him mention a place, the Trucker, which was halfway between Oshawa and Trinity. She wanted to understand, she needed to understand what was upsetting the life of her boyfriend so much. If they wanted to be a real couple, if they wanted their relationship to get real, to become something lasting, she didn't want to be excluded from a part of his life, she didn't want secrets between them.

Two weeks before, Steve had taken her to his workmate Andy's home and she had met the beautiful family of his colleague — his wife and his charming daughter — a simple but real family, like the one she was dreaming of having one day, maybe with Steve. It had been a pleasant evening, they had had dinner together and they were chatting and laughing when... Steve's phone had rung and he had changed completely from the pleasant self he had been up to that moment to a nervous, irritable person who had discussed on the phone and then had not been able to go back to the pleasant conversation of a few minutes before. After a short while they had left. He hadn't talked in the car while he was driving her home, he had been moody and visibly angry, she didn't know why and he didn't want to explain. Then he had called her the following day to apologize, he was sorry and he promised nothing would again ruin their time together, but when she had asked him to explain what had happened, what had changed his mood so abruptly, he had said the sentence that by now she knew by heart, even before he uttered it, "Please, stay out of it." The only thing he had added was that he was having problems with some people but that he would soon find a solution and go back to a normal life. But this normality was far away, judging from his behaviour that had changed from having a pleasant time together, then a phone call and... romanticism was over; only rarely they had had an entire evening without interruptions and the situation was getting even worse, the phone calls more frequent and menacing.

Now she was driving to the Trucker, she intended to find out what he did there and what kind of company he had. She prayed all her fears and her suspicions would prove groundless and that Steve had just had some meaningless discussions.

She arrived at the parking lot in front of the diner and she immediately saw that it was not a decent place; there was a coming and going of evil-looking faces and women who were clearly prostitutes. She parked her car and waited a few minutes. She had expected a bad place, but not so bad. She had never entered a similar place and she resisted the urge to turn her car and go back home. While she was recovering from the shock, she saw Steve's car arrive. He parked on the other side of the parking lot and clearly he had not seen her, because he got out of the car and started to walk towards the bar.

Jill braced herself, she took a deep breath and got out of the car. 'Now or never,' she thought.

"Steve," she called out.

Steve turned with a panicked expression on his face. "Jill, what are you doing here?"

"I wanted to see for myself where you spend your time without me!" A note of sarcasm was in her voice, even if at that moment she was more desperate than ironical.

"I told you, I implored you to stay out of it," Steve's voice sounded exasperated. "Why did you come here? We were supposed to meet tomorrow…" his voice trailed off, they had arrived at the door and he stopped.

"Why don't you introduce me to your friends now that I am here?" In reality she just wanted to run away, but she didn't know exactly what she should do.

"Go home, Jill, go home, please!" The door opened and a couple of bad guys came out, they saw Steve and they told him,

"Aren't you coming? We are waiting for you to start."

Steve was visibly embarrassed and he was torn between his so-called friends and his bad habits and this sweet, beautiful girl who offered him a normal righteous life.

He made a gesture to the men that meant, 'I am coming!'

Now he had entered the diner and Jill had followed him. She faced him and said,

"It's up to you, Steve. You can remain here and you'll see me no more or you can leave with me and we can go somewhere else to spend a pleasant and romantic evening together!" She knew she sounded harder than what she was in reality, but she was desperate and she was realizing now that she was in love with this man! Yes, she loved him! And she cared for him!

"You can't be serious, Jill!" He was trying to keep his voice low because there were still a few people and he didn't want to be heard. "I come here just to meet some friends. I don't have to give you any explanation for what I do and for how I live my life." He knew he didn't mean what he was saying. Jill was the person he cared for, the person that could save him, but oh, how difficult it is to say what you really want to when you are not free, free from vices, free to live as you like to, because you have built your own prison of lies, of vices, of debts, of bonds with people who will keep you in their power.

Jill felt she had no hope of forcing him to leave, she just turned and left... All the way back to Oshawa she cried desperately and she hoped that Steve would come back to her to ask for help, to explain, to make things right.

***

Father Mark had noticed something strange in Angela Dawson's behaviour when he had introduced Maria to her colleagues. He didn't like asking personal questions; his teachers, the students and his staff members knew that they could come to him whenever they needed to talk about their problems or if something worried them and that he was always ready to listen and give advice. Almost every day there was someone in his parlour; a parishioner, a student, a parent, a teacher, and he never said he didn't have time for them. Whoever talked to him could also count on his absolute discretion and what was said in that parlour remained in that room. When he knew that someone had a problem, he never failed to ask once in a while if everything was OK, if that relative had recovered, if that young student had found his way, if that difficult situation had been solved and he remembered everyone's needs in his prayers. This was his way of interpreting his role as priest, pastor and director of a school.

Now, he simply asked Mrs Dawson, "Angela, are you OK? Are you worried about something? I noticed you were a little distracted today at the meeting."

Angela blushed. She didn't feel ready to talk about THAT thing, even to Father Mark, not yet, at least. The only people who knew were her husband Tony and her sister Annette and they had promised not to tell anybody.

"Thanks, Mark. No, I am not worried. It's just something from my past that sometimes comes back to haunt me. Maybe one day I will tell..." A lump in her throat prevented her from explaining further. Father Mark didn't press her, he looked at her, smiling and said,

"You know that you can always come to me to talk."

She nodded and said, "Thank you. Mark, pray for me because, sooner or later, I will have to take a decision and it won't be easy."

"I will pray for you, Angela, don't worry, you are a sensitive woman and you have an affectionate husband. You will certainly take the right decision." And he left to go to the church for the evening prayer, knowing that Angela would come to him eventually when she was able to talk.

Chapter 4

Tuesday, September 2nd

Maria had spent a wonderful Labour Day with three of her new colleagues: Gloria, Melany and Francine. They had driven to a nearby town on Lake Ontario, while her colleagues' husbands had gone to the baseball game in Toronto. Gloria was fifty and she had two adult children who lived and worked in Ottawa, Melany was forty and didn't have children and Francine was forty-five and she had a sixteen-year-old daughter, Julia, who spent the afternoon with them. On Sunday, Maria had gone to walk at the lake with John and Greg, the sports coach; John was the same age as Maria, he had a girlfriend who was a nurse at the hospital in Oshawa so she was often busy on Sunday, Greg was forty-five and he was married to Barbara, the Latin teacher. They had met at Miracle High School and they had been married for five years now. Barbara had not been able to come on Sunday because she was babysitting her little nephew, her sister's son. Maria found all her new colleagues really kind and they planned a dinner at Maria's bungalow the following Saturday; everyone wanted to taste Maria's lasagne and tiramisu. Maria wanted to invite

Angela Dawson too, even if she was a little worried about her reaction the first time they had met.

Today Maria had to start her lessons at Miracle High School. Even though she had received encouragement from her workmates, she was really nervous when she left her home for the school. It was the beginning of a new life, but also of a new career. She would teach three levels of Italian Language: the first level with fourteen-year-old students, the second intermediate level with fifteen-year-old boys and girls and the upper intermediate level for the oldest students. The intermediate and upper intermediate were the classes that worried her most because they had had another teacher the previous years, Mrs Driscoll, and Maria knew from experience that it was always difficult to take someone else's class, especially if that someone was loved and admired by the students. Today she would start from the upper level so her anxiety was even greater.

The school day began with a blessing in the hall and the performance of the National Anthem. This was not done in Italy and Maria reflected that this habit of beginning the day with a homage to your country was really important because young girls and boys could learn from an early age to love the place where they lived and to respect it.

The corridor leading to the classroom seemed incredibly long to Maria, and at the same time, inexorably short, because beyond that door a new experience was awaiting her. She had been waiting for this moment for so long that she still didn't know if it was only a dream, but at the same time, she knew that beyond that door there was either the reward for many years of study, of practice, of sacrifices, or the disillusionment of an experience that would not be worth all her dreams. She longed to meet her new students, to get to know something about their young lives, their personalities, but at the same time, she was afraid of the possible difficulties, of the inevitable challenges that a teacher must always face when dealing with young people. She stopped in front of the door, then she gathered all her courage and she turned the doorknob. The classroom was fairly large, and just in front of the door, there was the teacher's desk so she slowly walked towards it, conscious of about twenty young students that were studying her, forming their first opinion of their new teacher. She put the register and her books on the desk and turned to face the completely silent class.

She smiled and said, "Good morning, my name is Maria Busati, I come from Italy and I arrived last week in Canada. In fact, it is the first time I have ever been to Canada. I am looking forward to getting to know you, and remember, I will teach you Italian, but whenever you need to talk to me about anything, I am always ready to listen. I have always been available for my students and I like to be considered as a teacher, but also as a person who can understand or who does her best to understand your problems or your opinions."

The young people in front of her were listening intently. Maria didn't know anything about their previous teacher who was much older than she and maybe preferred to keep a distance between her and her pupils because, from the young faces in front of her, she could perceive that what she had just said was new for them. But this was her way of being a teacher, this was her way of dealing with students and she always started her first lesson with similar words.

She opened her register and she did the roll call, stopping at every name and asking the boy or girl to briefly introduce himself or herself in Italian. She noticed that their use of the language was fairly good, with some minor mistakes due to the influence of their mother tongue. At this stage, she decided not to correct but to let students speak freely.

Before her first lesson, she distributed a sample of a CILS Italian test, the exam prepared by the University of Siena for foreign people for the different levels standardized in the European Framework. She gave them a level B1, just to check their general knowledge of the language. She noticed that they took the test seriously and she was happy to see that they were used to working with attention and dedication. She didn't want to mark this test, but when they had finished, she corrected it with them so that they could see what they had done wrong and make a kind of self-assessment.

After the test, she decided to explore their knowledge of Italy as a country, she projected on the interactive board a physical map of Italy and gave some general information about the characteristics of the peninsula, inviting them to add any information they had. Then she projected a map of Canada and they described it to their teacher. They were eager to describe their home country. Maria recognized a real love for Canada and she explained that now they could understand how exciting and motivating it was for her to talk about her country and culture.

After letting them intervene and talk freely, she asked them to work in pairs and create a list of vocabulary useful to describe a country and its physical features. The lesson went on smoothly and Maria felt that teaching came naturally to her and that these students were really motivated and eager to learn.

She realized that the lesson had ended only when she heard the bell because time had really flown by.

She said goodbye to the students, advising them to review the vocabulary they had learned before the next class.

While she was putting her books and her register in her bag, she saw two young girls who had remained in the classroom and evidently were waiting to talk to her. She smiled at them and said, "I am sorry but I have not learned your names yet."

The girls laughed happily and one of them answered, "Hello, Miss Busati. We just wanted to say that we liked your lesson very much and that we love everything about Italy and Italian culture. We are so happy to study in your class. My name is Meg." The girl who had just spoken was slim with brown eyes and auburn hair, she was dressed simply but with taste and her eyes reflected her excitement. She was an exuberant, lively girl but she was very polite in her manners.

The other girl was not very slim and she had green eyes and blond hair. She was wearing expensive clothes and she was clearly timid and less vivacious, but she was smiling and she nodded while her friend was speaking.

She said simply, "My name is Louise, I love studying Italian and I hope I will be able to remain in your class, because my dad…" Her voice trailed off and she cast her eyes down. Maria perceived a hint of sadness in her voice.

Meg turned to her friend and said immediately, "Oh, but don't worry, Louise, I will talk to your dad, if it is necessary, and convince him that he must respect your choices. He can't force you to study what he wants. Miss Busati…" Meg turned to the teacher who was silently listening to the conversation, "Louise's dad would like her to study Economics but she doesn't like that subject and she prefers languages and literature."

Maria was watching Louise's troubled expression while her friend was talking and she said, "Louise, I don't know your parents and surely your dad means well when he tries to convince you to choose a subject, but maybe you can ask him to talk to me. Try to tell him sincerely that you love what you have chosen to study and he will certainly understand."

Louise didn't look at all convinced but she smiled and said, "Oh, but this time he can't oblige me to do what he wants. He is not in his company where he can give orders and everyone obeys without discussing." Maria didn't like the belligerent tone of the girl but she also noticed that neither Louise nor Meg had mentioned Louise's mother.

She said tentatively, "Maybe your mum could talk to your dad. What does she think?"

She understood immediately that mentioning Louise's mum had not helped because Louise looked even more uncomfortable and said, "Yes, I will talk to them both. Thanks, Miss Busati, now we have to go home. See you!" Meg said goodbye to their teacher and the two girls left. There was something in Louise's words that disturbed Maria. She decided to wait and talk to the two girls again, maybe to Meg alone, so that she could better understand the family situation of Louise.

***

Meg always had dinner with her mum, Grace, and her dad, Andy, when her dad came home from work. He worked at Kilton Motor Company. She cherished her time with her parents in the evening because they spoke about what they had done during the day, and if there was a problem or they had a decision to take, this was the moment to discuss and talk. Grace and Andy were proud of their young daughter who was their only child and they saw her grow up an intelligent, generous and sensitive young woman.

Meg adored her parents who were for her an example and a guide, especially her dad, who sometimes helped her with her Maths assignments. She had chosen to study Mathematics because her dad was an accountant and an auditor in a company and she considered whatever her dad did the best.

Tonight Meg was particularly excited after her Italian lesson and the meeting with her new Italian teacher.

"Mum, Dad, I hope you will meet Miss Busati soon. She is really awesome and she speaks perfect English. Oh, how I wish I could speak Italian like that!" There was admiration in her voice.

Grace and Andy were always interested in what their daughter told them, always ready to listen and support their girl.

"Oh, we would have liked to go to Italy on our honeymoon," Grace said dreamily, "but it was too expensive at that time. Where is your teacher from?"

"She is from Padua in the north. We saw on the map that it is near Venice and there is an important university where Miss Busati studied. She showed us pictures of a wonderful church painted by Giotto — I don't remember the name — but it's marvellous!"

"There must be something beautiful and historic in every part of Italy, I think," said Andy. "Who knows, Grace, maybe we will be able to visit Italy one day!"

After dinner, Meg showed them the handout of the CILS exam and she explained to them the various exercises. After dinner, Meg and her dad helped Grace to wash up and tidy the kitchen and then they sat in the living room to watch TV.

Every evening, Grace asked her husband if everything was OK at work, even if she knew immediately when something was wrong because Grace and Andy were a couple that didn't need to talk, there was such a deep understanding between them that they perceived immediately if the other had worries and they couldn't hide anything from each other.

Tonight Andy said, referring to the colleague who shared the office with him, "Steve is nervous these days. I hoped that that girl he introduced to us would give him a little stability and serenity, but today, he was on the phone and they were not pleasant calls. He was angry and then he was distracted and agitated all day. I don't know what to do because I would like to help him, but when I ask him what is wrong, he just says that he has problems with some people and that I don't need to worry!"

Grace said, "That night we spent together with... I think Jill was the name of the girl, was pleasant but after the phone call he received, he was not the same and they left immediately. I noticed Jill was upset, maybe she knows something... I think, Andy, that you must leave him to deal with his problems and respect his wish to be left alone, but we must be ready to support him whenever he asks for our help!"

"You are right, Grace! There is no way I can help him if he keeps me at a distance!" Andy looked worried, but after a few minutes, he relaxed with his family and the cosy atmosphere of his home prevailed.

***

Louise left her friend Meg and went home. She lived in a beautiful villa that immediately revealed the social status of her family; her dad, Brian, was the manager of the Kilton Motor Company and he was what you would define a successful man, because he had made a fortune out of a business he had inherited from his father and he had been able to make it much more prosperous. He was not a nice man, he was an unscrupulous business man. He lived with his wife and daughter but he was often away on business and they had a housekeeper, Katie, who lived with them and took care of the house, the cooking and looked after Louise when her parents were not at home. Brian's wife, Susan, did not work but her days were almost entirely spent shopping, going to different clubs -- she belonged to a bridge club, to a golf club, to a tennis club — posting stories on Instagram and Facebook, making video calls, going to the hairdresser, the beautician, the manicurist, the physiotherapist, the personal trainer…

Tonight the family gathered at dinner. Katie had prepared delicious food as usual and they were all sitting around the table: Louise's dad and mum on opposite sides and Louise between them. Her mother had her mobile phone on the table next to her and kept on looking at it, her dad was reading the newspaper and Louise was eating silently.

She was so excited about her new Italian lesson that she said, hoping to arouse her parents' interest, "Today I started my Italian lessons." No reaction from her parents. Her dad raised his eyes from the newspaper and laid it on the table, her mum was texting someone on the phone. Louise went on, "We have a new Italian teacher. She comes from Italy and she is very nice!" Her dad's comment would have discouraged anyone, but not Louise who was used to similar remarks.

"It is high time that school hired an Italian teacher to teach Italian! That old teacher, Mrs Driscoll, surely couldn't speak properly and didn't know anything about Italy!" Louise's mum laughed at that remark and nodded.

"You are right, Brian, and that teacher was too old to teach anyway!"

Louise loved Mrs Driscoll but she thought that maybe having an Italian teacher would be an incentive for her dad to let her study Italian, so she went on,

"She comes from Padua not far from Venice. I would like you to meet her!"

Her father looked at her as if she had asked him for something impossible. "Meet her! Do you think I have time to come to see your teachers? I have a company to manage. And I have already told you, this year, whether you like it or not, you must study Economics. Susan," his wife reluctantly raised her eyes from her mobile, "you have to talk to Father Mark about Louise's choice of subjects. I need her to study Economics because I want her to work in my company in the future."

"But Dad, I want to become a teacher! I don't want to work in a company and I feel I wouldn't be able to be a good manager! Mum, say something to Dad, please!"

But her mother's phone rang and she went to talk in another room, without caring about her daughter's pleading words. Louise was really sad and disillusioned so she stood up and went to her room without finishing her dinner, knowing that no one would look for her or would come to see if she was all right. Looking out of the window after a while, she saw her mum all dressed up leaving… She threw herself on the bed and started crying. In the end she had studied Italian for two years now because her parents didn't have time to discuss it with her, but she felt lonely, almost as if she didn't have a family at all. When she was so sad and discomforted, she called her Uncle Joseph, her dad's brother and his wife, Isabel. They were so different, they didn't have children and they often spent time with Louise.

Now she picked up her phone and dialled her uncle's number:

"Hi, Louise!" when she called him at this time it meant that she was sad. Joseph had already tried to talk to his brother but he had simply replied that he brought up his daughter as he thought right. He was so different from his brother that, when their father had died leaving them the company, he had sold his share to Brian and he had opened his own accountant's office. He knew that his brother was greedy and he had a vain wife who only cared for luxury and expensive entertainment. He also knew that not all Brian's dealings were legal and so he had decided to stay far from it. He seldom visited Brian or his family but he frequently spent time with Louise whom he loved like a daughter.

Louise tried to sound cheerful while she told Joseph about her new teacher and her new lessons. Joseph knew that his brother didn't approve of his daughter's choice of subjects but he also knew that he was too busy to contrast her openly. Now he encouraged her and tried to cheer her up, letting her talk to his wife and showing interest in what his niece was telling them.

When she ended the call, Louise felt much better. Her uncle had promised her to meet her Italian teacher and she felt relieved. This phone call had been able to give her the warmth of a family. Sometimes she wished her dad and mum were her uncle and aunt. She sighed, texted her friend, Meg, for a few minutes and went to sleep serene.

***

Maria was preparing to go to bed and she was tired but she had started the habit of writing an email to Father Giulio every week and she didn't want to miss her 'appointment' with one of the dearest friends she had.

'Dear Giulio, this email will be short because today I started my school year and I am really tired. My first impression is very good. Today, I had my first class with intermediate and late intermediate learners and they are both interesting groups of students, motivated and enthusiastic. I spoke to two girls from the upper

intermediate class, Meg and Louise, they were nice and they stopped me after the lesson to say they like Italian culture. Louise must have some problems at home. I will eventually talk to her friend, Meg, or to Father Mark to see how I can help her because I had the impression that her dad would prefer her to choose other subjects. She is very kind and she seems motivated and it would be a pity if she had to abandon the Italian class!

Last weekend I spent some time with a few of my new colleagues. They are all nice and it's wonderful to walk on the path along the shore of the lake, here it is still warm and we have had sunny days. I enclose some photos of my walk and my excursion with my workmates yesterday.

I hope you are all right, thanks for your messages and your constant prayers. Love,

Maria'

Chapter 5

Monday, September 8th

Steve started the new week with a positive attitude. The previous Thursday night he had been finally able to talk to Jill. He had driven to Oshawa after work and he had waited in front of her home until she had opened the door and let him in. They had talked for a long time and it was the first time he had been able to recount everything that he had done up to his meeting with Jill; all his vices, his gambling, his debts, his obligations to people who helped him pay what he owed but who wanted something in exchange, his desire to be finally free from all these bonds. He had mentioned names and places. Maybe he had talked too much, he reflected now, and he had mentioned names that he shouldn't have, but he had realized that Jill was the girl he wanted to share his life with, a normal life, but that he needed her to trust him — there shouldn't be secrets between them if he wanted her to help him change his life.

Now he had finally made up his mind. In a few days, he would be able to pay his last debts, then... no more Trucker, no more gambling, just plans for a life with Jill.

On Friday, he had not gone to the Trucker, he had gone to the cinema with Jill, on Saturday they had gone for a walk on the lake, on Sunday they had gone to the baseball game. Three normal days. Why had he not been able to live a life like that before? When had he gone astray? When had he started gambling and playing cards and billiards with those bad guys?

A few more days and he would be free. No more debts, no more bonds. He was really serene today and he was glad when Andy, his colleague, noticed his change of mood and said he was happy to see him less nervous and more relaxed. Maybe one day he could invite Andy and his family to have dinner with him and Jill and celebrate his new life?

***

While Louise was going home from school, her Uncle Joseph called her.

"Hi, Joseph!" she said cheerily and he was happy to hear that she was not sad.

"Hi, Louise, we wanted to know if everything is OK with your school!" He always said 'we' because, even if he was alone while he was calling, he included Isabel in his concern for his niece.

"My lessons are very interesting this year, especially the Italian lessons. Our teacher, Maria Busati, has even given us some recipes of Italian dishes. Katie has promised to try them with me." She changed the tone of her voice when she added, "As expected, my dad hasn't mentioned my subjects any more, but last week he was particularly busy and he spent some nights away on business trips. I have decided not to bring up the issue of my school. If he is interested, he is going to talk to me about it!"

Joseph knew that his brother would not discuss it with his daughter, he would just oblige her to do what he wanted if he wished, but he was also aware that Brian would never 'waste' his 'precious' time going to talk to the teachers or to take a definite position about his daughter's school. Neither he nor Susan had ever gone to the school celebrations, the school play or the mass at the beginning or the end of the school year. Sometimes Joseph wondered why his brother and his sister-in-law had had a daughter, because he had never seen them play with Louise when she was a toddler or talk to her in a tender fatherly and motherly way. The few times they had been invited to his brother's, it had been painful to see the unsuccessful efforts of Louise to attract her parents' attention and the complete indifference and even annoyance of Brian and Susan. That was the reason why Isabel and Joseph had decided to spend as much time as they could with their niece and she had become more and more attached to them.

"Louise, I am glad to hear that you are happy about your school. Isabel and I will be on holiday for a couple of weeks, as every year in September. We are leaving next Thursday and we are coming back on the 25th. We are going to Vancouver to see Isabel's sister who has just come home from hospital."

Louise knew that her aunt's sister had had a serious operation but that everything had gone well and she would be back home soon. She was sad when her uncle left for his holiday in September because, when they had left for a cruise in August, she had gone with them and it had been a wonderful time. In September she was at school and she couldn't go with them. But she tried to sound glad when she commented, "Oh, yes, I know! Give all my love to Isabel's sister. I hope she is better. Can't we meet before you leave?"

"Yes, I was calling to invite you to have dinner with us next Wednesday so you can tell us about the news at school and about your teachers!"

"That's a wonderful idea! See you next Wednesday, Joseph, a kiss to Isabel!" Louise didn't bother to ask her parents for permission, partly because they always allowed her to spend time with her father's brother, and partly because they never asked what she was doing or whom she was seeing. They just knew she went to the gym twice a week in the evening, on Tuesday and Thursday, she went to the mass on Saturday evening and then she went for a pizza with her friends. They had never objected when she had told them she would spend the day at one of her friends' homes and Louise was not sure they even knew the names of her friends. She often envied Meg, who was not rich and didn't have a beautiful villa with a swimming pool, but had a real family, a dad and a mum that were always there for her whenever she needed their support, who always knew where she was, who were interested in her projects for the future and respected her decisions. All Louise's schoolmates were convinced that she was lucky because she had a lot of money and she could buy whatever she wanted, but she would have given her villa and her money in exchange for a mother and father that CARED for her!

***

Maria had had a really busy first school week and a pleasant weekend, and now, at home and with a cup of coffee in front of her, she sat down and took out her laptop to see her emails.

She was glad to see that a few of her Italian colleagues had got in touch with her and she answered their emails briefly, inviting one or two of them to visit her in Canada whenever they wanted. Maria was always polite and kind to everyone, but when it came to choose her close friends, she was very selective. Her colleagues or the people she met in her parish on Sunday in Italy did not know anything about her personal life, about her suffering due to her mom's behaviour. She hadn't told anyone of her father's letter, apart from Father Giulio. She was not shy, she was just reserved and maybe she had not found yet a person whom she felt she could trust implicitly. Even during the time of her father's illness, she always tried to smile at school, both in class and during meetings, and many colleagues had not realized that her dad was so seriously ill. On the other hand, she was always ready to listen to other people's problems and she never refused a few minutes of her time when she felt that the person in front of her needed comfort or advice. At school and in her parish she was respected and well accepted but she couldn't say she had a best friend or a person she trusted more than the others. She was not a loner though, because she enjoyed going to a pizzeria, a cinema or to a concert with colleagues or friends. But she was not similar to many of her colleagues who felt lost if they had to spend a day or an afternoon alone at home. She appreciated solitude and moments to stay by herself, listening to music, reading a good book, walking in nature and thinking.

The email that was always particularly welcome was Father Giulio's. He had written the previous Saturday a message full of affection, sending her pictures of a path in the countryside, amazing in the early Autumn colours. It was a path where she liked to walk with her dad when he still felt like it and was strong enough and then, alone, immersed in nature and in her thoughts.

Now she finally had time to answer and to tell Father Giulio about her first school week.

'Dear Giulio, thanks for your kind email and the photos that bring me back to Italy for a moment and to the beauty of its nature. The landscape is wonderful here as well and I have enclosed some pictures of Lake Ontario at sunset seen from the path not far from my home.

My first week at Miracle High School was really exciting and I must say I am satisfied of my approach to my new students and of their attention to my classes. Most of them are enthusiastic and they have asked me to bring them photos of Italian monuments and some Italian recipes to try with their families. I have shown them the 'Cappella degli Scrovegni' in Padua with the famous frescoes by Giotto and they were really enchanted by the beauty of the colours and by the way the great painter was able to capture the spirit of some episodes of the life of Christ.

My new colleagues are very nice. Last Saturday they were here in my bungalow for dinner. There were seven of them and I had to buy some chairs! We had a wonderful time and I am proud to say I cooked delicious lasagne and tiramisu. I hoped Mrs Dawson, the secretary of the school, would come, (I told you in my previous email that she was so kind when I arrived here!) but she said she had already been invited by her sister. It is strange... when we met at school she reacted as if she had seen a ghost or as if she had suddenly remembered something unpleasant. I hope I haven't said anything that may have hurt her. Now she is very kind but it is as if she wanted to keep me at a distance... Maybe it's just my imagination and she is timid or she is going through a difficult period.

Anyway, one of my colleagues, Julian, the Maths teacher, who is very nice, offered me his mother's car. Unfortunately, she has recently had heart problems and she doesn't feel like driving any more; the car is almost new, it is not very big, and you know, I don't like big cars. Last Saturday, I went with him to his mum's, she let me try the car. It is very comfortable and easy to drive, even if I have never driven a car with automatic transmission. This week we are going to make the transfer of ownership. With a car I will be more independent if I want to visit other places at the weekends.

Father Mark told me to say hello to you for him. I have learned that he has had health problems recently, but now he seems to have fully recovered. He is really a wonderful person, always joyful and encouraging with everyone, and even if he pretends not to, he is always aware if someone has a problem or looks sad... he notices everything, he watches over us and our students like a father.

I hope you are all right, Giulio. I keep in my heart your advice and I remember you in my prayers. I will keep you up to date.

Love, Maria'

***

Before closing his garage in the evening, Bill made a phone call; he didn't like the person on the other end, always so bossy and arrogant, but business was business and that person paid him well and he also paid Steve's debts every one or two months, so he couldn't complain.

"Damn it, Bill, I have told you a hundred times not to call me on my mobile. I have given you the number of the prepaid phone. Anyway, is everything ready?" the tone was never different, always nervous, always menacing.

"Yes, I have done the job you asked me. When are you sending someone to take everything away?"

"I think tomorrow, let me know how much I owe you, but nobody must know that I use your 'service,' so to speak."

"OK, OK, you have already told me. Steve is the only one who knows and he better not tell anyone. By the way, is Steve sick or something? I didn't see him at the Trucker last Friday, I tried to call him all weekend but he did not answer. What's the matter with him?"

Silence at the other end for a few moments.

"I didn't know anything about this. I saw him today and he looked calm and he was OK. Call him. You have to check on him, you know!"

"Why are you so nervous? I have just asked because it was the first time I hadn't seen Steve on Friday and the Friday before there was a girl with him."

"A girl? Who?"

"I don't know, but she did not belong to the Trucker, if that's what you are asking. I have never seen her before."

"We must be sure Steve doesn't back out. Call him! I have had doubts about him for some time now. He is too nervous. Does he still have debts with you and your friends?"

"Yes, of course. As long as he owes us money he doesn't want to back out or do some stupid things, you can be sure!"

"I hope you are right! Make sure you are right, or…"

The phone call ended abruptly, but Bill was used to it and didn't mind. He closed his garage and went back home.

When he was at home, Bill picked up his phone once again and made another phone call, but this time HE was the one who commanded, HE was the one who controlled.

"Hi Steve," he said immediately when the other person picked up the phone.

"Hi, Bill," nervous tone, even agitated. "Why are you calling me?"

"Last Friday I didn't see you at the Trucker. I tried to call you all weekend and you didn't answer. You are not thinking of going to the police, are you?"

"Of course not, I am not stupid! But I want to put an end to all this. I will stay in the game until I have paid my debts, but then I want to be called out."

"I don't think it will be so easy, you know too much about a lot of things and I am afraid you'll have to stay in the game."

"We'll see, Bill, we'll see."

"See you at the usual place next Friday?"

Steve ended the call without answering. Maybe he was being reckless, talking like that to a person like Bill. But Bill was right about one thing; was it so easy to back out now? Would he ever be free? It had been so easy to fall into the trap, but now? Who could he ask for help? He couldn't go to the police because he was in pretty deep, and in the last few years, he had moved away from all the people who could really help him. He didn't want to involve Jill because it could be dangerous for her and he cared too much.

The day that had begun so well was ending with fear and apprehension.

Chapter 6

Monday, September, 15th

Louise had spent the weekend at Meg's because her dad was in Ottawa on business, her mum was in Toronto with her friends and Katie had asked for two days off to visit her sister in Montreal. She had spent a pleasant weekend with Meg's family; they had gone to have a picnic on the lake on Sunday and on Saturday evening, after the mass, she had gone with Meg and some friends to eat a pizza in the new pizzeria downtown. At the mass, they had met Miss Busati and the Maths teacher and they had both thought that they made a beautiful couple; the good-looking Italian woman and the athletic dark-haired Canadian man. Miss Busati had stopped to talk to Meg and Louise and they had been tempted to ask them if they wanted to go to the pizzeria but Meg had thought that surely they had other plans for the evening. Meg and Louise liked the Maths teacher, Mr Stone, who was always smiling and was very patient with his students. They knew he lived alone next to his old mother on the other side of the town, not far from the motorway and they had often wondered why he didn't have a girlfriend because they thought he was attractive and pleasant.

As usual, neither Louise's father nor her mother had called to ask if she was all right and they had not answered her texts. Instead, she exchanged messages every day with her uncle and she knew they had arrived in Vancouver (they had sent her some pictures of the town from the airplane), Isabel's sister was OK, even if she was still weak after the long hospital stay. They had sent her a picture of them with her aunt's sister and her husband, Jon, and she had sent them pictures of Meg's family at the picnic and of the evening in the pizzeria.

On Sunday afternoon, Meg and Louise had studied together and had done their homework. They enjoyed doing homework together because they had the same method and the same way of organizing the school work. Louise had slept at Meg's and now they were going to school, chatting cheerily and making plans for the following weekend.

***

On Sunday evening, while Meg and Louise were studying, Andy had helped Grace in the kitchen and Grace had taken the chance to ask her husband, "You look worried this weekend, Andy. I have seen you distracted and not your usual self. What's the matter? Problems at work?"

Andy had smiled at his wife and said, "I can't hide anything from you, can I?" He had sat down on the sofa next to his wife and he had sighed, before saying, "Yes, I think a tough week at work is awaiting me, because I have discovered some irregularities in the account books I was revising. There are some shortfalls, some money that is registered and then disappears, some dealings that are not with the usual suppliers and are not properly recorded. I noticed something like this a few months back, but after a few days, everything seemed in order, so I thought I had been mistaken, but now… I have to talk to Steve about it, maybe he knows about some new suppliers and some dealings that he recorded while I was on vacation a month ago. There is certainly an explanation."

He had kissed his wife tenderly and she had asked, "What about Steve? You told me last week that he seemed more serene and calm? Is he still seeing that girlfriend?"

"Steve is really strange at the moment. Last Monday he was really happy, he called his girlfriend during lunch break and everything seemed all right then, the following day, he was nervous once again, he didn't talk much, he kept looking anxiously at his phone, he received one or two of those unpleasant calls. I really don't know, but I think he is struggling between his girlfriend and his past acquaintances, that are far from recommendable. I hope he will make the right choice!"

The rest of the evening had been spent pleasantly because Andy's family was for him a shelter, a refuge where he could relax and forget problems or difficulties, as long as those problems didn't touch Meg and Grace, of course.

Now he was at his office and he was waiting for Steve who often arrived a little late on Monday. Steve came into the office and he was visibly irritated about something but Andy knew that he had to talk to him because the things he had noticed in the account books were important. He had checked them once again this morning and the irregularities were there, he had not been mistaken.

"Steve, please, come here. I want to show you something on my PC." No matter how nervous Steve was, he was always kind to Andy, because it was impossible to be nasty with him. Andy was never rude. Andy always cared about everybody in the office, he had kind words for everyone and everyone loved him.

Steve stood behind Andy who was sitting in front of the computer and leaned forward to see what Andy was showing him. He was glad his colleague could not see his face because he turned pale when he realized that he had inadvertently registered something that he shouldn't have, while Andy was on vacation. Now, what could he do to hide it? Andy was a wonderful man, but he was too honest to pretend he had not seen it and he would certainly go to the manager, Mr Kilton, and then? He had to anticipate Andy's moves, that was the only thing he could think of in a few seconds.

"Yes, Andy, I see! I don't know what is wrong," he said tentatively. "Are you sure you didn't make a mistake in the data recording?"

Andy answered politely, even if he didn't like the idea that Steve was trying to blame him, "I have checked everything twice and I am sure I am not mistaken. I thought maybe while I was on vacation, you inadvertently…" his voice trailed off because he saw Steve's angry look. He had never seen his colleague look at him that way.

"While you were on vacation with your family," Steve knew that what he was going to say was unjust, but again, he was not free to say what he really meant, to behave in a natural way and tell Andy that it was all his fault, that he was responsible. Plan B his partners in crime had thought of was to lay the blame on Andy, who was the auditor for the company and the time for this plan B had come, because of Steve's mistakes, because of Steve's reckless life. "…While you are on vacation with your family, I have to do my job and yours, every year for two weeks…" Andy was looking at him unbelieving. "But I am sure I didn't make any mistake. Anyway, go and talk to Kilton, if you like." He had to prevent this at all costs, he knew.

Andy tried to remain calm, even if something was telling him that it was not just a matter of a mistake in the account statement, "Steve, I think you are overreacting! I didn't mean to question your work, which has always been impeccable. OK, I'll talk to Kilton and you'll see that everything will be settled."

But Steve said immediately, a little kindlier, "I will talk to Kilton next Thursday because now he is on a business trip for a few days and on Thursday night he will be in Oshawa at the convention. You know that whenever he is here I see him because I deal with the suppliers and the supplies and I have to report to him every week. Don't worry, we'll settle everything. If Kilton asks to speak to you, I will tell you, OK?"

Andy didn't know why, but he didn't trust Steve completely this time. Anyway, he thought that if he didn't hear from the manager, he would go talk to him personally in a few days. So he agreed and went back to his work, even if he was disturbed all day by Steve's reaction and by his harsh words of a few minutes before.

***

Maria's weekly email to Father Giulio had become a sort of habit. She realized it was Monday and she was opening her laptop to write to the Italian priest and friend.

'Dear Giulio,

I would like to write more frequently but time flies and my lessons keep me very busy. I must say that I am very happy about all my classes, from the beginner level to the upper intermediate. Next Saturday, I am meeting Mrs Driscoll, the Italian teacher who has just retired. Father Mark has put me in contact with her and I am going to her home. I hope she will give me some advice because I think experience is essential in the job of a teacher.

When I arrived in Canada I thought that my weekends would be lonely, but in reality I am never alone. Last weekend I met Julian, the Maths teacher, the one who sold me his mother's car, at the vigil mass and we went to a little restaurant with a terrace on the lake just outside the town. We had a very pleasant evening. Julian is a nice person, he is thirty-seven like me and he offered to take me to Toronto.

So, yesterday I had my first visit to the metropolis, a wonderful town, not chaotic at all. I went to the top of the CN tower. It was amazing. There is a glass floor and you can see the town below. I have enclosed some photos for you to see. We saw the Rogers Centre from the outside, the stadium with a retractable roof that is in the centre of the city. It is an impressive building and Julian promised to take me to a baseball game one of the next weekends, before the end of the regular season.

I enjoy the company of Julian, he is very polite and kind, but when I talked to him a little about my mum's behaviour I had the impression he didn't understand, he just said set phrases, like, 'Your mum certainly loved you!' 'Maybe she was not able to express her love to you,' 'You mustn't talk about your mum like this!' Maybe, Giulio, my situation is too difficult, too complicated for an outside person to understand and I am asking too much of Julian, who has an affectionate mum who adores him. Of course, I didn't talk to him about the adoption.

Anyway, we had a pleasant time together, I enjoy his company and he seems to enjoy mine. This week, with my most advanced class, I will talk about the 'borghi' the little towns in Italy that preserve, better than big towns, the traditions and the aspect of a medieval place. I have noticed that these students are eager to see photos of Italy, to get in contact with real-life material, not just what they find in their schoolbooks. It is really pleasant to talk to them, to help them discover my country.

Last week we read the Italian national anthem and we listened to it because here, every morning before the beginning of the lessons, they pray and listen to the Canadian national anthem. It is a tradition that we should have in Italy too, I believe, don't you think?

That's all for now, thanks for the photos you send me every week and for your affection that is important to me, because it is what keeps me connected to my past and to my home country.

Love, Maria'

***

Steve knew he had to make a phone call and he was incredibly nervous. After all, he would be calling a person who controlled and scared him, who could ruin his life.

After work, he went to the supermarket to do some shopping and then he went home with a heavy heart. Now things were really getting complicated and he started to doubt whether he could break the bonds and finally be free. He had avoided the 'Trucker' and his 'friends' for two weeks and he had spent more time with Jill, but now? What he had feared for many years had finally happened and this could mean the end of all his dreams of a normal life.

As soon as he arrived home, he picked up the phone and dialled a number he knew by heart. An arrogant voice answered, "Who's speaking?"

"It's me, Steve!"

"What's the matter, Steve? You know I am busy!" These were his so-called friends; no friendly tone, no friendly questions, but he was used to it and this was not the worst part.

"My colleague, Andy, noticed something in the accounts. I must have made a mistake and recorded something I shouldn't have while he was on vacation!"

"It's your business. You know what you must do. And you must do it quickly!"

"But isn't there another solution? I can't do this to my workmate!"

"It's your problem, not mine! And be careful! I wouldn't like you to become an obstacle to my business!"

"OK, OK! I will do what we have planned!"

The call was interrupted abruptly and Steve remained with the phone in his hands for a few minutes. He would have liked to cry but he was so exhausted he didn't have the strength to vent his despair. He felt lonely, and hopeless, and all the freedom he was dreaming of achieving was far, far away and unreachable. Jill could not help him, and at this point, she had better stay away from him.

He even thought for a moment of committing suicide. He was a good-for-nothing, nobody would miss him and Jill would find another man, much better than he was. But no, he didn't have the courage for such an extreme action. No, he must find a better solution, maybe he could talk to Andy. His workmate was such a sensible man, together they would work something out. But again, no, it was not fair to involve his colleague in something he, only he was responsible for.

That night would be a long one for Steve.

Chapter 7

Thursday, September 18th

Steve Brown's hand trembled as he dialled Andy Cooper's number on his cell phone. The time it took Andy to answer seemed an eternity to Steve who kept wondering what his colleague's reaction would be.

"Hello! Steve, is it you?"

"Hi, Andy." Steve was trying hard to keep his voice calm and to talk normally. "Listen, I am still in the office, I have talked to Mr Kilton about the irregularities you have seen in the account books and he wants to see us both in his office… NOW!" He knew his voice sounded far from calm and composed but he couldn't help it. On the other end of the line was the most honest and irreproachable person he had ever known and also one of the few real friends he had. He had already done something he was ashamed of.

"Steve, what's the matter? I don't think a few irregularities are something you should worry about, I am sure we'll settle everything with Kilton. But isn't Kilton in Oshawa tonight? And why not talk tomorrow morning? I am at home and I am helping my daughter with her homework."

"I am sorry, Andy, but the boss has changed his mind because he had some papers to check tonight and he is still here. He has told me tomorrow he has to go to Toronto on business and he wants to settle this thing as soon as he can. Please, I think it is a matter of a few minutes."

"OK," answered Andy reluctantly, "if you promise it will be no more than five minutes, give me the time to take the car and come to the office."

"I will wait for you here." Steve Brown closed the phone call and put his mobile phone on the desk next to his computer, thinking of what he was going to say to Cooper and hoping he would understand and help him. Or was it asking too much from a straight person like Andy?

Andy looked at his wife who had listened to his end of the phone call and was looking at him perplexed. Steve had never been so agitated, even in the most complicated times of his life. What was wrong with him? And it was strange that Mr Kilton was still at the office at this time of the evening.

"Do you really have to go back to the office at this time? Can't you talk to Kilton tomorrow?" his wife, Grace, asked him apprehensively.

"It will only be a matter of a few minutes and I will be back. You have nothing to worry about. Kilton can't blame anything on me, he knows I have always done a good and thorough job." He gently kissed his wife on her forehead and he told his daughter, Meg, to go on with her homework and they would check it later together. He didn't like to go out at night because he enjoyed the moments he shared with his family. Just staying with his wife and daughter after a day at work made him feel at peace.

He went to his car which was parked in front of his small house and he drove away, still wondering what had upset his colleague and friend so much.

He often asked himself why two such different people as him and his colleague, Steve, could be always on good terms and even be friends as they had two completely different lives. Andy was a family man, scrupulous in his job as an accountant in the Kilton Motor Dealing Company and devoted to his wife, Grace, and his daughter, Meg. He was proud of his only daughter who was such a pretty, sweet girl, always helpful and reliable and so wise and sensible for her age. She was sixteen and got good marks at school. His wife was a sensitive woman who worked as a waitress in the local diner but only part-time because she didn't like being far from her home and her family.

Steve Brown, instead, was not married, he sometimes said he had a girlfriend but his romantic stories didn't last more than a few weeks. He liked playing cards and gambling with some friends that Andy would never invite to dinner, they were far from his idea of an acquaintance. Andy knew Steve was always short of money because he heard him talk on the phone to people who were evidently angry at him and sometimes he looked worried. One thing that Andy always appreciated about his colleague was that Steve never forgot a little present for Meg on her birthday or some flowers for Grace on their anniversary. They rarely went out after work for a drink together and they seldom met outside the company where they worked, but Andy considered Steve a good friend. A few weeks before, Steve had gone to Andy's home to introduce his new girlfriend to Andy's family. They had had a pleasant night and Andy liked that girl, who was so different from Steve's previous female partners.

As far as their job was concerned, they got on well together, they had never had any argument. They were both good accountants and they respected each other.

When he arrived at Kilton Company, he parked his car in the deserted parking lot. Only Steve's car was there but he knew that the boss had a garage in the basement for his car so he wasn't surprised. It was strange for him to be there after working hours and there was a strange silence around him that made him feel uneasy. For a moment he thought of going back home but then he was a man of his word, and once he had promised to do something, it was impossible for him not to keep his word. So he got out of the car and slowly approached the dark building.

***

Steve was getting more and more restless as the minutes passed. He began to pace the floor of his office thinking of the best way to talk to Andy. One thing he knew for certain was that he really couldn't do what they had commanded him; he couldn't betray his colleague's trust and their friendship.

Why had he never been able to settle down, find a good wife and have a family? This would have helped him to stay away from bad company and from people who only dragged him further and further down towards his ruin. Why couldn't he be like Andy, who had someone to go back to in the evening, someone who trusted him, who made him feel serene and accomplished?

He walked out of his office, stepped into the corridor and reached Mr Kilton's office. He wanted to be sure the manager had left. The large room was empty, his boss's computer was off and there was no jacket on the coat hanger, so Steve returned to the office he shared with his colleague and turned on his computer because he wanted to show something to Andy when he arrived.

After a few minutes, he heard footsteps in the deserted corridor and he called out, "Andy, I am here in our office." He thought, 'What will Andy say when he discovers that Mr Kilton is not waiting for us and I have invented this excuse to be sure my friend will show up at a time when he doesn't like to leave his home? What will he say when I tell him what I have done and what they have ordered me to do?'

He turned to face the door of the office and he saw a dark silhouette in the doorway. He didn't have time to think of what was happening, he certainly didn't expect THIS thing to happen and he stared blankly at the shining blade that was going to hit him... Just a moment and then... a pain in his chest, blood... and... darkness!

***

Young Agent Moore answered the phone and heard a muffled and unnatural voice on the other end. At first, it was so low that he had difficulty understanding what the man (he was definitely a man) was saying.

"Hello! Trinity Police Station! Who's speaking?"

"Shouts and noises at the Kilton Motor Dealing Company! Some lights on the first floor are on! Come at once!"

"Excuse me! What did you say? Who is speaking?"

The voice repeated the message a little more clearly and hung up the receiver.

Chapter 8

Thursday, September 18th

Andy still couldn't believe what had happened in just a few hours. He looked around the squalid empty room where he was confined, waiting for Detective Grant. He was sitting on a chair behind a large table, in front of the table there were two more chairs and this was the only furniture. The walls were painted grey and there was a large glass partition but he couldn't see what or who was behind it. He had only seen a similar room in his favourite investigation series on TV. He was alone in an unnatural silence after all the voices, sirens and noises he had been surrounded by just some minutes before. He had completely lost track of time. Steve Brown had called him at eight p.m., he was at home, just after dinner and he was enjoying a peaceful evening with his family, his favourite time of the day. Oh, how he wished now he had not accepted to go back to the office, how he wished he had not yielded to the insistence of his colleague. He had sensed there was something wrong and he had not listened to the entreaties of his wife and daughter to stay at home. He had arrived at the office at eight-thirty p.m. and then…

everything was a blur in his mind; the body, the knife, the police officers, the handcuffs, the arrest, the drive in the police car. And now, he was there, at the police station, handcuffed, treated like a criminal and facing days of questioning, accusations, a trial and... He rested his arms on the table in front of him and placed his forehead on top but he wasn't able to cry, he kept thinking of his wife and child. Would they believe he was guilty, was the normal simple life he cherished so much gone forever? Desperation was seizing him, he had heard a lot of talk about the detective, Jason Grant, the head of the Homicide Squad, who was known as a tough man. He didn't take part in the life of the community, he was always taciturn and nobody had ever seen him speak or give confidence to anyone. Andy was a little afraid of talking to him but he hoped the detective would believe his words because people said that he had brought many criminals to justice and he was very good at cracking cases, even the most complicated ones.

***

Jason Grant was relaxing at home at nine-thirty p.m., watching TV and drinking a beer, as he did every night when his job as head of the homicide squad allowed him when his phone rang. He lived alone on the outskirts of the little town of Trinity in the house where he had moved from Toronto a few years before. Even if, because of his job, he was often called to other towns to investigate, he didn't mind because he liked his job and he had gotten used to thinking that his work was his life. He had lost all interest in meeting people and entertaining relations a few years before when his life had dramatically and drastically changed. What had not changed was his determination to bring criminals to justice, his firm conviction that drug dealers, murderers or people who caused the suffering and death of innocent victims didn't deserve any pity or any attempt to justify their deeds. When he talked to Father Mark, the director of Miracle High School, they often discussed this because the priest believed that there should always be a second chance for anyone, even the most hardened criminals, while Jason thought that some crimes which involved cruelty and a disregard for human life could not be forgiven and no second chance should be granted to these criminals.

Jason was a tall man in his early forties, he was slim and he had dark-blue eyes and short, curly, dark blond hair, slightly receding at the temples. Even if he seldom smiled, his face was not hard and he had a way of looking at people that was not devoid of sweetness. He had a congenital problem with his vocal cords and his voice was slightly hoarse. This contributed to his image of a tough policeman but when he spoke to the victims of a crime, especially children or women, he was incredibly soothing. All the agents at the police station considered him a great detective because of his devotion to his job and his intuitive abilities. Everyone trusted his opinions because he was seldom wrong when he detected lies in testimonies or when he pointed at a suspect as the culprit. His colleagues had learned to leave him alone. All their invitations to join them after work for a drink or a chat had been unsuccessful and they had stopped asking him, knowing that he simply preferred to stay alone especially in the last six years after his terrible loss. Everybody at Trinity Police Station knew exactly what had happened while he was working in Toronto even if he had arrived in the little town only four years before. They knew that he had a picture on his desk in his office, the picture of a young girl smiling happily, but nobody at the police station had ever dared to talk about that smiling girl or ask him questions or even express their sympathy to him. The only person he sometimes went to visit for a chat was Father Mark, who had known him since he was a child and who was the only person he talked to about that sweet, smiling young girl who was always in his heart.

When he answered the phone after lowering the TV volume, he knew that something was wrong because nobody called him at night just to talk to him. The voice on the other end of the line was professional and quickly brought him up to date with the latest events at the Kilton Motor Company. The Kilton Motor Company was the local car dealer. Jason had met Mr Kilton only once, and personally, he didn't like him because he knew some people who had bought a second-hand car from him and had been far from happy with it. The Kilton Motor Company was not far from the motorway in an industrial area on the outskirts of the town. Jason, instead, lived not far from the lake in a pleasant district immersed in nature but a short walking distance from the centre of Trinity.

Jason didn't hesitate, his duty came first. He got ready in a few minutes. He always dressed casually in a shirt and jeans with a leather jacket or a blazer. He drove to the scene of the crime. When he arrived, he parked his car in the parking lot next to Andy Cooper's car and he entered the building where the lab technicians and the forensic team were already at work. The coroner came to him immediately and led him to the office on the first floor where the victim, Steve Brown, lay in a pool of blood not far from the door. Jason knelt down and examined the body.

The coroner explained that Brown had been stabbed in the chest by a person that stood in the doorway. He died immediately.

The agent who had arrived first on the scene recognized the unmistakable voice of his superior and approached him.

"Hello, Jason, sorry to disturb you but I wanted you to see the scene before we take the body to the morgue! We were alerted by an anonymous call at eight-thirty-two p.m.! The voice said that movements and shouting were heard inside the Kilton building and that there were lights on the first floor. We couldn't trace the phone call because it was too short and came from a prepaid phone that is not registered. When we arrived, the building was deserted. The only light on was in this office. When we entered, we found the body of Steve Brown as you see it and a colleague of the victim, Andy Cooper, was next to the body with a blood-stained paper-knife in his hand, in a state of shock. He was not able to give any explanation and we took him to the police station. We hope that, by the time you get there, he will have recovered from his shock. All the evidence points at him, of course, at least for the time-being."

While the agent, David Hogan, was talking, Jason looked around the office. When David finished relating the events to him, he said,

"Tell the technicians to take all the computers in the office to the lab. I want to know everything about this company and the job of the victim and the suspect. I want you to investigate the life of the victim from every possible angle and to learn something more about the relationship between the victim and the suspect."

"Of course, boss!" Jason looked at him disapprovingly because he didn't like to be called 'boss'. David noticed this but he continued,

"We called Mr Kilton as soon as we arrived here but he is out of town, he is in Oshawa for a convention of car dealers and his wife told us that he is coming back tomorrow morning."

"OK! Are there any witnesses apart from the anonymous call?"

"No. We didn't find anybody in the vicinity of the building; the only cars parked were the ones of the victim and the suspect. All the lights were off except the one in this office, and at this time, the company is usually deserted."

"I think I will go to the police station to talk to the suspect, Andy Cooper, before they take him to prison. There is something about this whole business that doesn't add up, there is something that I can't quite understand. Why were these two employees here? What were they doing? I need more information before accusing one person!"

Jason knelt once more beside the corpse of Brown, he looked at it for a few minutes, then he stood up and ordered it to be taken to the morgue for the autopsy. He took leave and went back to his car. Before driving to the police station, he made a phone call to his trusted friend and his first 'informant', Father Mark.

"Hi, Mark, sorry to disturb you at this time."

"Hi, Jason. Don't worry, you know I am always available for you. What's the matter? Are you OK?" Father Mark had a particular affection for this tough police officer who had a great burden on his heart he had not been able to overcome yet. He knew that he was in reality a good and upright man who had been hardened by his great loss.

"I am OK, Mark, I have just been called to the Kilton Car Dealer for a homicide. One of the employees, Steve Brown, has been killed and I am now going to the police station to interrogate the suspect who was found on the scene of the crime, Andy Cooper. I know that you are very reserved and I can trust you with this information. Am I wrong or have you mentioned Andy Cooper once or twice in our previous conversations?"

"Of course, Jason. The first name, Brown, I think it was, is not familiar but the second one, Andy Cooper, is the father of one of our best students, Meg. He has a beautiful family, I see him whenever the parents of our students are invited. He sometimes helps me with the accounts of the parish and I really can't believe he is a murderer. His daughter, Meg, is the best friend of Louise, the daughter of Kilton, the manager of the company. I can ask if anybody in the parish knew the victim if you like?"

"Thanks, Mark, you know your help is always appreciated! Good night!"

"Good night, Jason, see you soon!"

Father Mark was really worried when the phone call ended because he knew Andy and his family very well and he was aware that Meg had the highest consideration for her dad, she really looked up to him as her hero. He prayed to God that Jason could exonerate him soon because he knew in his heart that Andy was innocent and he was aware of the effect that a similar predicament could have on a young teenage girl.

***

Jason arrived at the police station when it was eleven at night. He wanted to interrogate Andy Cooper before they took him to prison because he wanted some of his questions answered, at least, the first ones concerning the presence of the two accountants in the office at that time.

He went straight to the interrogation room where the policeman on duty told him that Andy was relatively calm and that he kept on repeating that he was innocent.

Jason entered the room and went to sit down in front of Andy. Andy was a handsome man, tall with blond hair and green eyes, he looked a little older than Jason, but now his upset face and dishevelled look reflected the shock he had had in the last few hours and his desperation. If he really was the murderer certainly Jason thought it had not been a premeditated act, because Andy did not have the countenance of a cold-blooded killer.

"Hello, Mr Cooper, I am Detective Jason Grant of the Homicide Squad. Can you tell me what happened tonight?" Jason's voice was professional and cold.

Andy looked at the detective with a dejected expression and it took him a few minutes to take heart and speak, and when he talked it was almost a whisper.

"I didn't do anything, Detective, when I arrived Brown was on the floor dead. Instinctively I took the knife. I was unable to move, and a few minutes later, the police arrived and found me there."

"Andy, I asked you to tell me everything that happened from the beginning," the policeman told him patiently and a little less coldly.

Hearing that he called him "Andy" made the suspect feel a little more at ease and helped him to collect his thoughts that were still confused.

"At about eight p.m. Steve Brown called me from the office at the Kilton Car Dealership where we both work as accountants. He told me that Mr Kilton wanted to speak to us both in his office. A few days ago, I told Steve that I had noticed some irregularities in the account books and that I wanted to talk to the boss at once, but Steve insisted on speaking to him. I agreed and tonight he was very nervous when he called."

"Was it normal for your workmate to stay in the office so late?"

"Absolutely not, I was surprised and I was even more surprised when he told me that Mr Kilton was waiting for us both in his office because the boss always left early in the afternoon. And this afternoon, in particular, he had planned to go to Oshawa for a convention of car dealers."

"That's what I was going to say, he can't have told you that Kilton was waiting for you because he is out of town and he is coming back tomorrow morning."

"I assure you that is what Steve told me. I made the same objection and he answered that Kilton had changed his mind, otherwise I would never have gone back to the workplace. My wife was listening to my end of the conversation and she can confirm what I am saying."

"Go on! What else did he tell you on the phone?"

"I have already said that he was nervous and that was strange because there was no reason to be. The irregularities were not so serious and I thought it was something we could easily settle with the boss the following morning. I told him so but he insisted, saying it was only a matter of a few minutes. My wife was perplexed and worried. She asked me not to go but I had promised Steve and so…" Andy had to stop talking because the thought of his wife and daughter took hold of him and he had to fight back the tears.

Jason was looking at him intently, and for some reason — call it intuition, experience, knowledge of human nature — he believed what this man was saying and he sympathized with him. He knew what it meant to have a quiet, peaceful life and suddenly to see it destroyed.

"What happened next, Andy? You must be sincere with me if you want me to help you," he tried to sound encouraging.

"I drove to the office and I entered the building. When I walked down the corridor that leads to my office and Mr Kilton's, I immediately noticed that the boss's room was empty but I thought he was in our office waiting for me, even if I didn't hear any voices. When I arrived at the door, it was open, and just beyond it, I saw Steve lying on the floor and I stumbled upon the paper-knife that was lying next to him. I inadvertently picked it up, then I knelt next to Steve but there was nothing I could do for him." Tears were rolling down Andy's cheeks and he started to tremble at the thought of his friend dead on the floor. "I am sorry for Steve, he was a good man and he was so lonely, but I swear I didn't do it! You must believe me, Detective!" he implored.

"Now try to keep calm and to remember, this is very important. Did you hear any noise in the building, did you notice anything when you entered and before you found your workmate? Even a detail that seems insignificant to you may be important."

Andy was at the end of his strength and all the emotions, all the events of these last hours were straining him but he tried hard to collect his thoughts and his memories.

"When I arrived, there was only Steve's car in the parking lot. I was not surprised because Mr Kilton has a garage in the basement for his car, but when I entered the building, I noticed the light in the reception console that indicates that the garage door is open. Maybe I am wrong but I am fairly certain that I saw it."

"Thank you, Andy, we will verify what you are saying. Did you notice anything else?"

"No, there was no one around and the building was deserted and silent. Whoever killed poor Steve had already left. He must have killed him between the time he called me and the time I arrived. I had to get dressed and it took me a quarter of an hour at least to drive from my home to the Kilton Company."

"OK, Andy. I know that you need a little sleep but I have to ask you one more question, OK?" Andy nodded, he was so tired and confused.

"What do you know about your colleague? You said he was lonely. Did he have any relations, friends, people who had something against him? Anything could be useful for us!"

"He always said that he envied my life, so organized and orderly. He had a completely different life. He was not married and he didn't have a stable relationship. He liked to play cards with friends or gamble and I know he always had money problems, but he was a good man and very competent in his job. He was always kind to me. I think he has a sister living somewhere far from here but he seldom heard from her."

"What about the irregularities you noticed in the accounts, Andy?" Jason knew he was pressing for information but he felt he had to learn as much as possible.

"I started to notice some discrepancy between the figures that my colleague, Brown, passed me and which seemed like a regular occurrence, and the data I found in the general database. I asked Steve for an explanation and he immediately became nervous. He offered to talk to Kilton and tonight he called me to tell me that Kilton wanted to see us both immediately in his office, which seemed strange to me, but Steve had never lied to me and so I did as he asked! Oh, I wish I had listened to my wife and daughter and stayed at home." Desperation was seizing him again and he looked at Jason who was standing up.

"Thank you, Andy, for having told me what you know. If you have been sincere and you didn't kill your workmate, you have nothing to worry about. We will get to the bottom and find the real culprit, you can be assured."

"I swear I didn't do it, you must believe me!" Andy said pleadingly. But… was he imagining it or did the detective nod just imperceptibly and smile at him? Did he believe him? He didn't dare to ask… but he prayed to God to help him and his family.

While Jason was driving back home, well after midnight, he couldn't help feeling pity for that man who had seen his life shattered in a few minutes. There were many things in the first reconstruction of the events that didn't make sense; first of all, the motive. Steve had called Andy and not vice-versa. Next, the anonymous phone call; Andy had told him that when he arrived he didn't see anybody around the building. The phone call must have been made when Andy was already in the office. But Andy said that he didn't hear shouts and he didn't notice any movement.

Jason was looking forward to start investigating the murder the following day because his instinct told him that they didn't have the culprit in prison.

Chapter 9

Friday, September 19th

Before going back to the Kilton Car Dealership the following morning, Jason Grant went to the police station to talk to David Hogan, the agent who had supervised the preliminary investigation on the scene of the crime the previous night. Before going to bed, he had called Hogan to tell him what he had learned from his conversation with Andy Cooper.

As soon as he entered the police station, they told him that David Hogan was waiting for him in his office. He entered the small room where he spent most of his days when he was not travelling for his investigations. Hogan was sitting on a chair in front of his desk. Jason went to sit opposite David just in front of a big window overlooking the lake.

"Hello, David," he said curtly. "What can you tell me about the murder? Have you got the results from the lab or the autopsy?"

Hogan was used to the brusque ways of his superior and he didn't mind; he admired Jason Grant, considered him a gifted investigator and trusted Jason's opinions on the cases, even if they contrasted with his own. He had learned that Grant was very seldom wrong.

"The result of the autopsy has not arrived yet but I think the cause of death is pretty obvious. The computer technicians have analysed the database of the two computers and the strange thing is that, in the files from Cooper's computer everything seems in order, while in the victim's files there are some irregularities. It is as if the shortage had been found by Brown and not by Cooper. And yesterday night, while we were searching Brown and Cooper's office we found two envelopes full of money in Cooper's desk drawer. This could give Cooper a motive..." Jason was listening intently to what Hogan was telling him because it was exactly contrary to what Cooper had told him the day before.

"Any fingerprints on the envelopes and the banknotes?" Grant asked.

"Too many fingerprints but the funny thing is that there are no fingerprints of Cooper. Maybe he used gloves... On the contrary, on the paper-knife there are only Cooper's fingerprints..."

Jason seemed perplexed and doubtful. He asked Hogan, "Did Brown have any relatives? I think Cooper told me last night that he has a sister somewhere..."

"Yes, he has a sister who doesn't live in Canada. She lives with her husband in England. We have called her and she said she would pay for the funeral but she could not come to Canada now because her mother-in-law is seriously ill. She seldom heard from her brother anyway."

"OK, I want you to investigate the life of Brown; it seems he was a gambler and always in debt. I want to know a little more about his way of living, his friends, girlfriends and so on. Have you talked to anyone at the Kilton Company?"

"No, yesterday night it was deserted and I thought you would go there today. This morning Kilton called and asked me about the investigation. I asked him if he knew anything about the money in the drawer and he seemed surprised. He said that Cooper, being the auditor, had access to the company bank account but he seemed not to believe him capable of subtracting money. Do you want me to go there and talk to him?"

"No, don't worry, I am going to the Kilton Company now. I have already called and they told me Kilton is back and he is waiting for me. Let me know what you find out about Brown."

"Of course, I will start immediately!"

While Hogan was leaving, Jason called him back, "David! One more thing…" Hogan retraced his steps to the office.

"Yes?"

"Last night, when you arrived at the scene of the crime, did you notice any lights on in the reception console?"

The agent thought for a moment before replying, "No, no light was on, why do you ask?"

"Oh, I just wanted to check on something. Thanks, David."

The agent left and Jason remained a little longer in his office. When he was sitting there he could not help but look at the beautiful face who was smiling in a frame on his desk. It was the photo of a pretty young girl, blond with green eyes, who couldn't be more than eighteen or twenty years old. He sighed sadly before standing up and preparing to leave.

***

Jason Grant arrived at the Kilton Company. In the daylight he could see the building and the surrounding property better than the previous night. On the corner of the road, there was a parking lot just for the employees in front of a big industrial building. Before parking his car, the detective made a tour around the block occupied by the structure completely. The ground floor was entirely surrounded by windows and it was devoted to the display of cars on sale. The other section of the parking lot was for customers, and near the building, there were rows of used cars. The first floor of the large structure was occupied by the offices of the employees and by the large office of the manager. This was the part Jason had briefly visited the previous night, the scene of the crime. The basement of the building was the garage where the mechanics fixed cars and there was a section where the manager kept his car when he was at work. There were two shutters at the rear of the building; one for the company garage and the other for the manager's garage. Opposite the garages, there was a popular gym where many people living in Trinity went. Apart from that, there were only industrial buildings around because this was not a residential area.

Jason parked his car in the customers' section and entered the building. The receptionist looked at him and he showed her his badge.

"Detective Jason Grant of the Homicide Department," he introduced himself in a professional tone.

"Mr Grant, the manager, Mr Kilton, has just arrived and he is waiting for you." Jason was looking at the big console with interest.

"When the garage shutter is opened is there a light on in the console?" he asked abruptly.

The receptionist looked at him and answered, "Yes, there is a light for the workshop shutter and a light for the manager's garage shutter." While she was talking, she showed Jason the two LEDs that were now off. "The light goes off when the garage door closes automatically," she continued.

"When you arrived this morning, do you remember if one of these lights was on?"

The receptionist didn't show any reaction to these questions. "No, no light was on, but no one uses the garage at night and Mr Kilton had left the office early in the afternoon yesterday to go to Oshawa on business."

Jason thanked her and took the elevator to the first floor. The company seemed to be working as usual, even if an employee had died and another one was in prison. Jason couldn't help thinking that it was strange or at least it was a little tactless but he didn't want to judge this behaviour, at least not before talking to the manager.

The manager's secretary met him in the corridor and led him to the manager's office. She was a pleasant woman in her fifties, of medium build and not very tall who wore large glasses and looked very professional. Jason stopped her before reaching Kilton's office door.

"May I ask you a few questions?"

The secretary, Alison Lewis was written on her name tag, became visibly nervous.

"Of course, but I was not here yesterday night and I can't be of any help. When I arrived this morning I learned what had happened and I am still shocked. Brown was always kind and friendly to everyone. We will certainly miss him…" After a pause, she added, "And Andy has always been so considerate and gentle to everyone, I can't believe he has killed his colleague."

"Can you tell me exactly what the main tasks of Cooper and Brown were? I understand they were both accountants but did they have specific duties?"

"Yes, Brown took care of the invoices and the supplies and he had contact with the suppliers and Cooper was the auditor and registered the data Brown passed to him."

"How many people work here?"

"There are five sales clerks and five people in the office, including me, of course. In the garage, there are ten mechanics, if I remember exactly."

"Thanks, Miss Lewis. Do you know if Brown and Cooper had problems, did they argue or quarrel?"

"I have never heard them arguing and they were always on good terms, I don't think they met outside the office, they led completely different lives."

While Miss Lewis was speaking, a tall man opened the manager's office door. He was a sturdy man in his early fifties, bald with a stern expression on his face and a general air of superiority and self-confidence. Jason thought that it was certainly not easy to work for him, because he had a certain way of looking at the secretary that was very off-putting and cold.

"Miss Lewis, I told you to usher the detective in, not to entertain him. You must be Detective Grant. Please come in."

Miss Lewis was certainly used to Kilton's manners because she seemed totally unfazed. "Mr Grant, this is Mr Kilton," she said smiling and she went to sit at her desk.

"Please, Detective, come in and sit down!" the manager said politely while he closed the door. Jason entered the office that was very large, with a big desk in the middle in front of the window, two tall bookcases on opposite sides of the room, a sofa in a corner with two armchairs and a small table next to the desk with a coffee machine and some mugs on top.

Mr Kilton went to sit behind his desk and invited Jason to sit in one of the armchairs opposite him.

"I am very sorry for the death of your employee, Steve Brown," the policeman started politely.

"We are all saddened and shaken and you surely have wondered why we are open today," Jason sensed the nervousness of the manager and his fear of the detective's judgment. "We had some appointments with prospective customers and I am waiting for the arrival of some new cars so I had to open the company even if I would have desired to close at least for a day of mourning out of respect."

"Mr Kilton, what time did you leave for Oshawa yesterday?"

"I left at around four p.m. I went home to pack my bag and I left for Oshawa. I planned to go to a meeting of car dealers in order to get in touch with prospective buyers and sellers. Since I was to finish late, I booked a room in a hotel and I came back this morning. My wife didn't call me last night to inform me because she knew I was busy and she thought it was useless for me to come back last night so I was informed by my secretary as soon as I arrived."

"Did you talk to Mr Brown or Mr Cooper before leaving, Mr Kilton?"

"Mr Brown called me a few days ago to tell me that he had noticed that Cooper was worried and he had heard him say on the telephone something about money taken from the company accounts. I told him to look into the matter and then yesterday he reported that he had discovered some irregularities. I asked him to call Andy Cooper and tell him I wanted to talk to him today to clarify things with him. Cooper has always been an honest man and a good accountant and I believed there would be a logical explanation for his actions, something we could easily work out together. But when I called the police station this morning, an officer told me that they found money in Cooper's office desk drawer, so I don't know what to think!"

"What about Brown? Did you trust him? Did you check the accounts personally to verify what he had told you?"

"Brown and Cooper have worked in this company for many years and I have never had any reason to complain about them or their work. They are very precise and thorough and I have always trusted them. Yes, I checked the accounts this morning after calling the police, and I am sorry to say that there was a money withdrawal from the company account signed by Cooper a few days ago. I would never have thought that he would be able to do such a thing. Certainly, he had a reason, maybe he needed money. What saddens me is why Cooper did not come to me to ask for help. I could have given him an advance to his salary."

"Thanks, Mr Kilton. I don't have any other questions for now but I would like to have details of your meeting in Oshawa, just to clarify all points in my report."

"Of course, my secretary will give you everything you need. If you'll excuse me now, I have to go back to work."

Jason's phone rang, he excused himself and answered, he listened for a few minutes and hung up. He turned to Kilton, who was already going to the door, and said,

"They have just told me that you have sent a lawyer to assist Cooper in prison."

Kilton was slightly taken aback but he recovered immediately and said with a pleasant smile, "To tell the truth, my secretary asked me this morning if we could send one of our lawyers to Cooper and I consented, even if it is not my custom to do these kinds of favours, especially if Cooper has taken money from the company! But as I have already told you, he has always been irreproachable until now and I know his family is not wealthy."

"That was very generous of you, Mr Kilton. You can go back to your business now, I am sure we will meet again soon," Jason said, but as he went back to his car, he couldn't help but think that he definitely didn't like Kilton and didn't trust him.

***

Maria was surprised when she didn't see Meg in class because she was one of her most enthusiastic students. Meg often stopped after her lessons to ask her questions and the teacher liked the young teenager. Louise, Meg's best friend, was in class but she was constantly distracted and it was evident that something was worrying her.

Maria didn't have time to talk to Louise after the lesson because Father Mark was waiting for her outside the classroom with a grave expression on his face, which was strange because he was always smiling.

"Maria, can you come to my office for a few minutes? I need your help."

"Certainly, is anything wrong?" The serious countenance of the priest was making her anxious because there was certainly something wrong.

She followed him along the long corridor to his office that was next to the staircase. It was a study with walls lined with bookcases, a big mahogany desk in front of the window with a big armchair behind it and two smaller armchairs in front of it. It was so similar to Maria's father's study that, every time she entered, she felt a wave of sadness, and at the same time, she felt instinctively at home. That room in her father's home was linked to so many memories of pleasant moments spent together with her dad, reading, discussing the events of the day or the news and enjoying the harmony and the love that they shared.

Seated in one of the armchairs, Maria immediately recognized her student, Meg, who had her face in her hands and was softly crying. Maria felt that something was terribly wrong with that sweet young girl, who was usually smiling serenely, so enthusiastic about her studies and so eager to learn new things; the ideal student every teacher would want to have in her classroom.

She went to her and knelt beside her, putting her arm around the teenager's shoulder. Meg immediately buried her head against her teacher's neck and went on crying, but now the sobs were shaking her and she no longer tried to restrain her emotions. Maria looked at Father Mark, who was standing on the other side of the desk, watching them. He shook his head slowly and said,

"Meg's dad was arrested last night for the murder of his workmate. Meg's dad and the victim worked in Louise's father's company. Meg didn't come to school today because she went with her mum to the prison to visit her dad, but just before your lesson ended, she came to me and asked me if she could talk to you. She has not been able to tell me much because, as soon as she tries to talk, she starts crying. I told her to sit here, hoping you would be able to calm her down."

Maria moved the other armchair nearer to the one where Meg was sitting and sat down so that she could keep on trying to soothe Meg. She gently caressed the girl's hair and waited patiently until the sobs started to subside. In the meantime, Father Mark had sat down on his armchair and was watching the little girl anxiously. He had dealt with teenagers for many years now and he knew how a predicament such as the one Meg was experiencing could affect the mind and the feelings of a young girl. He silently prayed for Meg and her parents who were facing this difficult time, because he was sure that Andy Cooper was not guilty.

"Meg, please, stop crying," Maria was talking tenderly to the girl. "I know it is hard but everything will be cleared and your dad will come out of prison sooner than you think, I am sure." While Maria was talking, Meg was shaking her head.

"You must be strong and support your mum now, Meg," Maria was going on, "she needs you more than ever before. And you are not alone. I am here whenever you need me and Father Mark is always ready to help you and your family, you know."

"Oh, Miss Busati, I don't know…" Meg was trying to speak but Father Mark and Maria sensed there was something terribly wrong, something more than what they already knew.

"Meg," Father Mark leaned forward on his desk, "You know your dad is innocent, you must only be patient and wait for the investigation to end and I am sure Detective Grant will find the real culprit. He is the best detective I have ever met," he added with a smile.

"No, Father Mark," Meg was trying to say something that weighed on her heart. "This morning, when we arrived at the prison there was a lawyer we have never seen who was leaving my dad." Father Mark exchanged a quick glance with Maria, alerted by what Meg was saying. He knew that Meg's family didn't have a lawyer because they couldn't afford one and he had already thought of offering his help, but why was a lawyer already there?

"Dad told us that Mr Kilton's secretary has asked her boss to send one of the lawyers of the company to help him because she knows that we can't afford a counsellor. The lawyer had just told my dad that the manager has found evidence of embezzlement in the accounts and that Brown had told him that my dad had taken the money. The police have also found envelops with money in my father's desk drawer in his office. So the lawyer advised him to plead guilty because, since there is no premeditation, he could avoid a trial and have a lighter sentence."

Here Meg couldn't restrain herself any longer and she started crying once again. It took her some minutes to calm down but her troubled face expressed all the worries, all the desperation, all the disbelief of this young girl who had seen her peaceful family life shattered in a night.

Father Mark spoke slowly but firmly, "Meg, I am absolutely sure your dad is not guilty. He is not guilty of embezzlement and he is even less guilty of murder, and you know that too. The lawyer certainly wanted to present your dad with the different possible scenarios, even the worst, but there will be surely another solution."

"My dad is confused, he is worried for me and mum and he seems so lonely there in prison without his family." Meg's words and her anxiety were really heart-breaking.

Maria said, "Meg, why don't you tell us what happened yesterday? Maybe if we retrace the events we can help you. Your dad is certainly innocent and I am sure that, in the end, the truth will come out."

"My dad told everything that had happened to Detective Grant last night and he said that he had the impression that the detective believed him. You know, Father Mark, many people here in Trinity think that Detective Grant is very tough because he never talks to anyone and he is very serious, but dad told me that he was not cold to him, he just asked him to tell him the truth. And today, the lawyer reproached my dad for talking to the police without consulting a solicitor."

"Meg," Father Mark didn't want to say that he had already talked to Jason, "Detective Grant can seem tough if you don't know him but I have known him since he was more or less your age and I can tell you that he is a fair man. If he treated your father kindly it means he doesn't think he is guilty, that's for sure!"

"But now even the detective must have seen the evidence the lawyer is talking about and my dad is sure that Grant has certainly changed his mind about his innocence!" Meg said, "If you know him so well, Father Mark, tell him to help my dad. I don't want him to say he is guilty if he is not!"

"He is not!" Father Mark repeated firmly. "You must never doubt this, Meg, never! Now, why don't you do what Miss Busati suggested; why don't you tell us what you know?"

The support of the priest and the teacher seemed to soothe Meg who now was not crying and seemed comforted by their words.

"Yesterday night, I was doing my homework and dad was helping me with Mathematics when the phone rang. Mum and I only heard dad's part of the conversation but it was Steve Brown, dad's colleague, on the phone. It was strange because he seldom called and never at eight p.m. after work. He asked dad to go back to work because Kilton, the manager, wanted to see them immediately about some problems in the accounts, I don't know what exactly. My mum just told me that dad was worried because he had found irregularities in the company accounts and he had had a discussion with Steve. Dad had never gone back to the office at that time and I sensed he was worried when the phone call ended and my mum was also perplexed, but Father Mark, you know my father, when he gives someone his word, he never changes his mind. And so he left, telling me to go on with my homework, that he would be back in a short time. Then we didn't see him come back and we were worried and then…" Her tears filled her eyes and she was not able to go on.

Father Mark didn't want to force her to speak further because he realized that remembering what had happened made the young girl suffer so much. He offered to drive her home so he could talk to her mum and offer her his assistance. The girl agreed and she thanked her teacher.

"Meg, I would like to come to talk to your mum too. I know she has never met me and I don't want to intrude at this moment, but if I can help your family in any way, please let me know!"

"Thanks, Miss Busati. I have already spoken so much about you and your lessons to my family! I was so happy with my studies, but if my dad goes to prison, I don't know…" Father Mark interrupted and said once more,

"Your dad will not be sentenced to prison, Meg! Just be patient and let the police do their job!" He turned to Maria and added, "Thanks Maria, I would like to talk to you tomorrow about this situation after I have spoken to Meg's mum."

"OK, I will do anything I can to help your family, Meg"

The young girl went down the stairs with Father Mark and Maria stood outside the priest's study watching them leave. She was worried for Meg. A young girl who sees her life devastated by such a terrible event must be supported and assisted because teenagers are so fragile. They are just making their first experiences and the family is essential for them because the parents are a reference point, a support and role models. She prayed everything would be cleared up soon!

Chapter 10

Saturday, September 20th

Father Mark had come back from Meg's home the previous day more and more worried about the situation. He knew that Jason did not like to discuss his investigation especially at the beginning, but he needed to talk to him and he needed to talk to Maria Busati too.

He picked up the phone and dialled Jason's number. He knew it by heart as he had called the detective so many times. He had met Jason for the first time in Toronto when he lived in the Salesian Community there. Jason attended the Salesian High School and he was a brilliant student and a pleasant guy, so different from the Jason Grant people in Trinity had met. But life can make you harden, especially when tragedy strikes! Jason had not changed in his devotion to his job, in his commitment to people in need and in his struggle for justice; he had just moved away from the company of other people, become introverted and solitary. Maybe, Mark reflected, he was afraid of growing fond of someone, because he believed that he could put the life of his friends and dear ones in danger, as it had happened so tragically a few years before. But Mark knew that his heart had not changed and he prayed that, one day, something or someone would find a way to soothe his pain and his remorse.

As usual, Jason answered almost immediately, "Hi Mark, how are you?" he always asked immediately how the priest was because a short time before he had had heart problems and he had to be careful.

"I'm OK, Jason. I know you are at the beginning of an investigation and I don't want to intrude, but I talked to Meg, Cooper's daughter, and her mum yesterday and I am worried about them."

"Mr Kilton told me yesterday that he has consented to send a lawyer to the prison to talk to Andy," Jason said. "The attorney has criticized him for talking to me the night of the murder and he has asked to be present whenever I talk to him. I am worried too because, even if Andy was frightened, he told me his story and he seemed sincere to me. I tried to talk to Andy's wife and daughter this morning but they were very reluctant to talk to me. They were clearly frightened and maybe they had been advised by the lawyer not to talk to the police."

"Jason, is it true you have found evidence of Andy's involvement in the irregularities in the company?" he couldn't force himself to say the word "embezzlement" connected to Andy, whom he considered the most honest person he had ever met.

"I am sorry, Mark, but we have found two envelopes with money in the drawer of his desk in his office and some documents for the withdrawal of the money signed by him.

Being the auditor of the company, he had access to bank accounts. The day before yesterday, he told me that HE had discovered irregularities and that Brown had called him and Brown's call was confirmed by Cooper's wife and daughter. There is something that I still don't understand."

"I am sure that Andy has not embezzled money and has not signed those documents. Someone is trying to frame him, but who?" The question was more to himself than to Jason. "His wife and daughter are frightened and they say that the lawyer is trying to convince him to declare himself guilty. This would be a great mistake! Jason, can't you talk to him once more?"

"The lawyer won't let me talk to him alone, but if you go, Mark, you will be allowed to talk to him privately and maybe you can convince him. If he is not guilty, it is a terrible mistake to confess to a murder he didn't commit, which will make it more difficult for me to find the truth!"

"I certainly agree with you, but what worries me is that Meg came to me yesterday sure her dad was innocent but when I drove her home to talk to her mum, they were starting to believe what that lawyer was saying. I am sure that, if the lawyer is able to convince Meg and her mum, he will convince Andy more easily."

"I know and I promise I will do everything I can to find out the truth even if he declares himself guilty. But if you have difficulty talking to Cooper's wife and daughter, who can?"

"I want to talk to Meg's Italian teacher. You know that we have a new Italian language teacher who arrived a few weeks ago from Padua. She has already impressed her young students and Meg asked to talk to her yesterday after she visited her dad in prison. Miss Busati is a talented teacher and she is wonderful at gaining the trust and admiration of her teenage pupils. She said she was ready to help and I want to ask her to talk to Meg and her mum. Maybe she can convince them to support their dear one's innocence."

"I think Cooper's family will need support and comfort, and if this teacher is so good at talking to people and putting them at ease, ask her!"

"Thanks, Jason, see you tomorrow after the mass as usual, OK?"

"OK, see you tomorrow then!"

Jason saw that his detective, David Hogan, was politely waiting for him to end the phone call. He opened the door of his office and let him enter.

He had asked David to investigate the life of the victim and he was eager to learn what he had discovered:

"Hi, Jason. I can say that our victim was certainly not an angel. He spent his free time in that diner on the motorway…" he looked at his notes because he didn't remember the name of the place, "…Trucker. It is a place for gamblers and prostitutes that our colleagues in that part of the town know very well. They have made raids, closed it down for a while, arrested some drug dealers but they always succeed in opening it up again."

"I think I have heard of it. Was Brown a gambler? Did he owe money to someone?"

"Yes, he was always in debt and you won't believe who one of the bad guys is who he owed money to?" Jason looked at him waiting for an answer.

"One of our old 'acquaintances,'. Bill Tucker"

Jason looked at him disbelievingly. "You mean Bill Tucker, the one who owns a garage not far from Kilton Motor Company? But that guy is a gangster. He has been arrested... how many times I don't remember, but he has been arrested for violence, drug dealing, riots..."

David Hogan knew Bill Tucker very well, one of his best agents had been wounded by Tucker, luckily, not seriously. Tucker had spent some time in prison and he had been released more than a year ago.

"Yes, that Bill Tucker. I have already sent for him but his workmate at the garage said he will come back next Monday morning as he is out of town 'on business.'. I have already asked him when he left and he said that he left last night, so he was in Trinity on the night of the murder."

"Be sure to pick him up at the garage and bring him in for questioning first thing on Monday morning. I want to hear what he has to say..."

Jason was convinced that, if Brown had associated with people like Tucker, the investigation would be much more complicated than he had thought.

He decided that it was time for him to go to the Trucker and talk to a few people there.

***

Alison Lewis should have enjoyed her Saturday as usual. She was not at the office and the previous night, after a day dealing with her boss, Mr Kilton, the police and with the phone calls from many people who wanted to know about the murder — journalists, customers and suppliers — she was really tired.

But she was restless and anxious today and she couldn't concentrate on her usual weekend chores: the shopping, the hairdresser, the cleaning and a relaxing walk on the lake, which was a thing she longed for.

When she learned that the policemen had taken those envelopes from Cooper's drawer she wanted to say something but then she reflected that she didn't know anything for sure. Mr Kilton had already been angry with her for talking to the detective and she didn't want to lose her job. She couldn't afford to lose her job because she had to pay for the nursing home where her mum was forced to live after the bad stroke she had suffered.

But she was tormented because it's one thing to say you don't want to be involved and another to convince yourself that this is the best thing to do, the thing that will allow you to live in peace with your conscience.

She was sure she had seen Steve Brown put those envelopes into Cooper's drawer and she was sure she had seen Brown in the company parking lot discussing with that disreputable guy, the mechanic, she thought she had heard him call him Bill. Was there any connection between the money, the guy and the envelopes? Should she talk to that Detective who seemed so cold and professional?

Finally, she made up her mind. Next Monday she would talk to Kilton and ask for his opinion about this matter. If Kilton had consented to send Cooper a lawyer so promptly when she had suggested it, it meant that he wanted to help him so he would be interested in her information, wouldn't he?

Now that she had taken a decision, she felt relieved and she could relax and enjoy her walk on the lake and her night at home watching her favourite program on TV.

***

Father Mark called Maria but she didn't answer and so he went to the church to pray and think. After a few hours, while he was getting ready for dinner, Maria called him back.

"Father Mark, I am so sorry I missed your call. I was at Mrs Driscoll's, I thought I told you I would meet her today. She gave me precious advice and information about my lessons." Mrs Driscoll had been the Italian language teacher for almost twenty years at Miracle High School and she had just retired. When Maria arrived in Canada, she was on a cruise in the Caribbean with her husband, but as soon as she had come back, Father Mark put her in touch with Maria and they agreed to meet today. He was glad Maria had been able to meet Mrs Driscoll; they were so different but they shared a love for their job and their students and he was sure the old teacher could be a great help to Maria.

"I am glad you have met. I had forgotten about your visit to Mrs Driscoll. Maria, I have to talk to you about Meg and her mum and the difficult time they are going through. I am really worried for them."

Maria immediately abandoned her enthusiasm for her meeting with the old teacher and for the pleasant afternoon they had spent together, and focused on her young student who was visibly suffering.

"I know that you met Meg's mum at their home yesterday. How are they? Meg is so attached to her dad and she is such an affectionate young girl, I can only imagine what she is going through."

"Meg and her mum are very confused. I know that having a lawyer is important when you are accused of a crime, but I believe that that lawyer is not giving them the right advice and he is a little too fast in drawing conclusions; maybe because he doesn't know Andy Cooper." Maria could feel all the anxiety of the priest in his voice which was usually cheerful. Now he spoke fast and nervously, trying to express his emotions and his concern.

"Tell me what I can do for them. Meg's mum doesn't know me yet and I don't want to intrude, but Meg has shown great interest in my lessons, she always stops me to ask questions. I had even promised that I would bring some photos of my hometown and my hikes in the Alps to show her. Maybe I could try to talk to them and understand what worries them. I wouldn't like them to start believing Meg's dad is really guilty."

"That is exactly my fear, Maria. I talked before lunch with the detective, Jason Grant, and he asked me to go to talk to Andy in prison and try to learn exactly what the lawyer is planning to do. I have called the prison and they have granted me a visit for tomorrow morning, before mass. Jason went to talk to Meg and her mum but they clammed up and were reluctant to talk to him. Jason is very professional and he may seem cold if you don't know him as I do, so I was thinking, would you mind stopping by after mass tomorrow to talk about this situation, after I have visited Andy? Then we can decide what is best to do, OK?"

Maria immediately agreed and promised to be at the ten-thirty a.m. mass, also because she had missed the vigil mass that she usually attended. Father Mark asked her how Mrs Driscoll was and he was happy to hear that they had spent an enjoyable afternoon together. He ended his phone call and reflected that Maria had really soothing qualities, not only on her students but also on a person like him, who had spent the whole day worrying and thinking. How was it that now he felt more serene and peaceful? That young lady was going to be a great help to him, he knew, for sure.

***

Jason drove to the Trucker in the late afternoon. The parking lot in front of the diner was not yet packed with cars as it would be in a few hours. Saturday night was always busy for places like the Trucker. People came to play cards, meet women and discuss their business. People who were certainly not to Jason's or Father Mark's liking, but rather, people who lived with activities bordering on the illegal or even overstepping those borders quite often.

Jason had arrived early because he wanted to talk to the owner. He parked his unmarked car and went into the diner. There were just a few people at the bar drinking beer and some people sitting at a table. He went to the bar and a man behind the counter came to him to take his order, but seeing the badge attached to his belt, he retreated immediately. The police were not welcome in places like this.

Jason called him back with a gesture, and reluctantly, the man came nearer.

"Hi, my name is Grant, I am a detective with the police. Are you the manager here?"

"No, if you wait a minute, I will call him for you."

"Thank you." Jason said simply.

The man went to the back of the diner, and a few minutes later, a big, burly man came out and approached the policeman. He had dark eyes and long, dark, greasy hair gathered in a short ponytail.

"Hello, my name is Smithson, Carl Smithson, what do you want here?" His tone was far from conciliatory and kind, but Jason was used to this type of people and he didn't expect a different reaction.

"Hi, I just want to ask you if you have ever seen this man," he showed him a photo of Brown on his mobile phone.

"Yes, he was a regular customer for some time. I heard he was killed a few days ago! I haven't seen him for some time now but he was normally here on Friday night with his friends."

"Can you give me the names of his 'friends'? Were they always the same?"

"Yes, they usually go to the other room to play cards or billiards and they stay all night until closing time on Friday and Saturday."

"How many people belong to Brown's circle of friends?"

"There are four, sometimes five, plus Brown, of course!"

Jason wanted to ask for the names of the people in Brown's company but he decided to wait until he had spoken to Tucker. Instead, he asked,

"Did you ever see Brown with a woman? Did he have any female friends?"

The man thought for a moment, "No, I don't think... But wait, a few weeks ago, Brown came in with a beautiful girl, not a girl that we normally see around here, if you understand what I mean!"

"Certainly, how often did you see him with that girl?"

"Only once, but they were arguing and she tried to convince him to leave. Finally, she got angry and left. At first, he looked as if he wanted to follow her, but then he stayed and went to play cards and talk to the other guys as usual."

"If she left and he stayed, it means they had not come together, I presume."

"Now that you make me think of it, you are right. They entered together but they were already arguing. Maybe they met in the parking lot."

"Didn't you hear a name?"

"No, I didn't." Jason thanked him and left. He went to his car and drove back to town.

***

Andy was led back to his cell after the lawyer had left. He had a sheet of paper in his hands and he looked ten years older than three days before.

When he was back in the cell he looked disbelievingly at the paper. The lawyer had left him a draft of a confession to sign and he had said he would be back next Monday to check it once again before presenting it to the District Attorney.

From what the lawyer had said, there was no possibility of his innocence being proven, because all the evidence was against him. He had been found near the victim with the paper-knife in his hands, two envelopes with money — exactly the amount that was missing in the account books — had been found in his drawer and the withdrawal documents had been signed by him.

The lawyer had insisted that one thing was 'positive'; there was absolutely no premeditation so the charge would be 'second-degree murder' and he could have a relatively light sentence if he declared guilt. This would spare him a trial and his family would not spend months attending long hearings in court. The attorney had particularly stressed the predicament his family would go through if he didn't admit his guilt. He was so confused, so desperate, so lonely.

But... there was something inside him that wouldn't accept the idea of declaring himself guilty of a crime he hadn't committed, not only the murder, but he had never signed those withdrawal documents and he didn't know anything about the money in those envelopes. There had to be someone who believed in his innocence, there had to be another way! That detective, Jason Grant, seemed to believe him but the lawyer had gotten so angry when he heard that he had talked to him and now he wanted to be present whenever he spoke to him!

The sense of rebellion that was lingering in his mind began to grow but then he saw his wife and daughter terrified and anguished at seeing him in prison, frightened and worried for him. 'Oh,' he thought, 'what shall I do? What is the best way?' At that moment he started to pray, "God, I have always tried to be a good Christian, help me. You know that I am innocent, you read my conscience and my heart, help me to do what is best for me and my family. Send me someone who can really help me, because I think that, only a person who believes I am innocent, can really support me!" The prayer gave him a little comfort, and as exhausted and desperate as he was, he fell asleep.

Chapter 11

Sunday morning, September 21st

Maria had never missed her mass every Sunday in Italy. When she was a child and a teenage girl she used to go with her parents and her sister, then, after her mum died, the Sunday mass had become one of the cosy traditions she had shared with her dad in the twelve years they had spent together. They went to the ten a.m. mass and then they stopped at a bar in front of the church for a cup of coffee or a cappuccino.

When Maria arrived in Canada, Father Mark gave her a small booklet with the holy mass in English and told her the times of the Festive Services. She would have liked to attend the ten-thirty a.m. mass because Father Mark celebrated it and she liked the priest and his simple way of addressing young people and adults alike and his serene view on life. However, the Sunday morning mass carried so many remembrances and so, she generally preferred to attend the vigil mass. The previous day she had been at Mrs Driscoll's and it had been such a pleasant visit that she had missed the mass. She also wanted to hear the news that

Father Mark would share with her after his visit to the prison.

When she entered a church, she couldn't help but feel the soothing and peaceful atmosphere and gratitude for all the joys and blessings the Lord had bestowed on her. At the same time, all the people who were suffering came to her mind. Today she was thinking of Meg and her mum; what a difficult time for a teenage child and a young wife who doted on their dear father and husband. She asked God to help them and to guide them in His infinite Grace and she prayed that Andy would be soon cleared of the crime of murder.

She sat in a pew in the middle of the church and she observed a tall man who had just entered. He was really handsome and he had an interesting face, very expressive. Beyond a first impression of hardness and gravity, Maria could see a sweetness in his gaze and she could perceive the attitude of a person who was used to suffering. He sat down next to her and nodded slightly at her with a small smile. She smiled at him politely and noticed the badge on his belt. She had learned that this was the way Canadian policemen wore their badges even when they were dressed in civilian clothes.

Was this the detective Father Mark had mentioned, the one that frightened Meg and her mum so much? Maybe he could make someone feel uneasy but she believed she perceived a great benevolence in him, a great sense of justice and of duty that she didn't dislike.

***

Louise was used to going to the vigil mass on Saturday evening with her friend, Meg, but yesterday evening she did not feel well and her parents had insisted on going with her to the Sunday mass instead. In reality, she did not want to meet Meg and her mum, because she didn't know what to tell them.

Meg was her best friend, they had always been schoolmates since elementary school and they complemented each other. Meg was always enthusiastic and extrovert, insatiably longing to learn new things, very good at school in every subject, but also generous and trustworthy; the friend everyone would like to have. Louise was shy and selective in her choice of friends. She was not so brilliant at school but she was a hardworking student. She always depended on Meg's encouragement and support because she was easily discouraged. Now life had changed their roles and Louise didn't feel able to be the one who encouraged and supported Meg, she didn't know if she could find the right words.

Louise had something else that tormented her; the night of the murder she was coming out of the gym that was just opposite the garage of Kilton Motor and she saw something… did she have to tell the police what she had seen? She had tried to talk to her parents, especially her dad, but he had got so angry that he had frightened her and he had ordered her to stay out of it. Her mum was texting her friends and had not listened. Maybe she could talk to

Uncle Joseph when he came back from Vancouver, but now? Maybe what she had seen was just a coincidence and didn't mean anything, but why didn't her dad want her to relate it to the police? Certainly, he had nothing to be afraid of... or... ?

Whom should she ask for advice? She could not talk to her mum, who refused to listen to her and never had time for her, maybe Father Mark... or, just in the pew in front of her, she saw the new Italian teacher, Maria Busati. She was so nice and she seemed so wise. She always spoke about the importance of the family in her lessons...

Maybe she could talk to her, maybe Miss Busati could find another way to interpret what she had seen that night, maybe there was another explanation...

Louise made up her mind to talk to her teacher after her Italian lesson the following day, and having taken her decision, she felt better and she started to pray that would be the right way.

***

Jason had only just recently started to attend the Sunday mass regularly again, in fact, he had started going back to church when he had moved from Toronto to Trinity. Father Mark had become director of Miracle High School in the little town, and when he had seen him after some years, he had immediately felt the comfort and support that priest had always been able to give him. His suffering, his sense of remorse for what he had experienced in Toronto had not vanished. After the Sunday mass, he had begun to stop by in Father Mark's study and talk to him, not necessarily about himself and his past, but more generally about the events of the week, his work and the people they knew. Father Mark asked him occasionally for help when he noticed a strange behaviour in one of the young people in the parish or the school and they had successfully guided some young girls or boys away from bad company and back to the safety of their families and a healthy life, far from drugs or vices. Father Mark never hinted at Jason's great loss; he knew that it always weighed on his heart but his support consisted of making Jason feel useful in the community, stressing his abilities as a detective and his qualities as a defender of justice and safety. Jason knew that Father Mark loved him as a son and that he sympathized with him. He admired and appreciated the priest for his wisdom and insight into the problems of young and adult people alike. He trusted the priest's judgment and his opinion and he appreciated his advice.

When he went to church, he had always questions lingering in his mind, 'Why, God, have You asked so much of me? Why have You chosen to give me such a great sorrow? Why this loss that weighs so much on my conscience? Will I ever overcome this? Will I ever be able to feel at peace with my conscience? Will I ever make peace with my sense of guilt?' He prayed he could find an answer to these questions one day. Father Mark used to tell him that God never abandons the people who have faith, but he had felt abandoned by God six years before, why had God permitted that tragedy?

This Sunday, he was on duty but he found the time to attend the mass; he also wanted to know what Father Mark had been able to learn from Andy Cooper in prison.

He entered the church and noticed a pew where only a young woman was sitting. He sat down next to her and he turned to see if she was someone he already knew. Because of his job and the small community of Trinity, he knew a lot of people there. He had never met this young lady, her smile when she turned to him, was friendly and sweet, she was a pleasant woman. He noticed that she had a small booklet in her hands with the English mass service, so he imagined that she was not English or Canadian. In a moment, he remembered that Father Mark had told him that there was a new Italian language teacher at Miracle High School and he had perceived that Father Mark appreciated her way of teaching and talking to teenagers. He could understand why she inspired trust in the people around her; her simple and genuine smile was really captivating and charming. He instinctively smiled back at her and prepared to follow the service.

***

Father Mark was a true man of God, his faith was always perceivable in his way of approaching people, talking about everyday life, in his sermons, his cheerful, and apparently, carefree behaviour, which was not carefree at all. It was just the behaviour of a person who put all his cares and the events of his life in the hands of God, who truly believed that only in God's Providence everything finds a reason and an explanation. This did not mean that Father Mark did not have his moments of doubts, anxiety or concern, especially when someone he knew was in trouble, but a moment of prayer, the rosary or the reading of a page of the Gospel always succeeded in soothing his fears.

One of the moments of his consecrated life that he preferred was, of course, the daily mass and the Sunday mass had a special meaning for him, because Sunday was the sacred day for every Christian and because the Sunday mass was his favourite chance to see all the community gathered in prayer and thanksgiving. After the mass, he liked the moment, outside the church, when he could meet the people of his community and everybody knew that, if they had a problem, this was the right moment to talk to the priest, he was always ready to listen, comfort and advise. In the last few years, since Jason had come to live in Trinity, after the mass, he liked to stay with him for the time that Jason's commitments allowed him to remain, but these were precious moments because he loved Jason, he tried to support him and to help him overcome his tragedy.

Now Father Mark was standing at the altar in front of the congregation and he watched them all with infinite love. He liked the image of the shepherd with the sheep. He knew something about every person who was in church, their endeavours, inner struggles, moments of sorrow but also the joys and the little and great successes and satisfactions they had.

He was happy to see Jason because he knew that he had had difficulties finding his way back to church and prayer, which was understandable, knowing what he had gone through, and for this reason, he was even happier to see him every Sunday. But who was standing beside him? Maria, the sweet Italian young woman who had had her share of suffering in her life. Father Giulio had talked to him about her dad, her past and he admired her even more for her wisdom, sensibility and affectionate relationships with her students. Seeing them standing side by side, the priest involuntarily smiled because they were two people in search of serenity and fulfilment in their lives, even if they both had rewarding jobs. Could God be guiding them to… ? Father Mark offered a prayer for them both because he never interfered in the feelings of his parishioners.

What was happening to Louise, sitting between her parents behind the teacher? He had rarely seen her parents at a mass before. Why did she look so upset? Yes, her best friend was in a moment of difficulty and anxiety, but why had she not gone to the vigil mass, where Meg and Louise usually met? Father Mark decided to talk to Louise in the following days to encourage her to support and comfort her friend, Meg.

His most fervent prayer today was for Andy, whom he had just visited in prison, and for his family. Only God could guide them in the way of truth and justice.

***

After Father Mark finished talking with his parishioners outside the church, he turned towards Jason and Maria who were waiting for him. Jason had just talked to a man and Maria had briefly said hello to Louise, who had quickly asked her if she could talk to her after the lesson the following day. Maria agreed immediately but noticed that Louise was talking quickly as if she didn't want to be heard by her parents and that they were hastily going to their car without stopping to talk to anyone. Louise thanked her teacher and hurried away.

Father Mark approached Jason and Maria and introduced them.

"Hi, Jason, this is the new Italian Language teacher I have talked to you about, Maria Busati. Maria, this is the Homicide Detective here in Trinity, Jason Grant. I saw you sitting next to each other in church."

Jason smiled and shook hands politely with Maria. Maria couldn't help but notice that his smile was warm, but at the same time, sad. She looked at him and said shyly, "Yes, I think Mr Grant noticed that I need your booklet, Mark, to follow the mass in English, even if I am starting to learn."

Jason immediately said kindly, "You mustn't be embarrassed, I would like to speak Italian as you speak English, Miss Busati. Call me Jason, please!" Maria noticed immediately the characteristic husky voice of

Jason, but she liked it because the low tone made it softer and kinder, she thought.

"And I am Maria, Jason," she replied pleasantly.

Father Mark invited them to sit in his study so that they could talk about Andy Cooper's situation in private. Jason and Maria sat down on the two armchairs in front of his desk while the priest sat opposite them.

"Excuse me, Jason, but before telling you about Andy, I want to ask Maria, I noticed you were talking to Louise outside the church. Why was she at the Sunday mass? She seemed upset and I can understand that knowing that she is Meg's best friend, but I am surprised she didn't go to the vigil mass where she could meet Meg and support her."

"Yes, I think she is very upset and she asked me if we can talk after my lesson tomorrow but I had the distinct impression that she was talking to me without her parents' knowledge and approval. But maybe they were just in a hurry," she added quickly.

Father Mark reflected for a few moments and commented, "Yes, I can understand it must be a difficult moment for Louise's family, too. After all, the murder was committed in her dad's company and Andy Cooper is his accountant."

"Maybe that is why she is so nervous," Maria said, "because her best friend is worried about her dad, but her father is involved in this matter too, being the manager of the company. Let's hope this matter will be cleared soon!"

Father Mark sighed and added, "Well, I wanted to stop Louise and talk to her, but since she asked to talk to you, I will wait..." he looked perplexed and added, turning to Jason,

"This morning I went to see Andy in prison and I am very worried about him because he is confused, upset and he doesn't sleep. He said that he can't eat and this situation is breaking his spirit, I am afraid. He said that his wife and daughter would visit him this morning too. Let's hope that seeing his family will revive him a little." Father Mark was really preoccupied and troubled.

Jason was looking at him and Maria could see that he was concerned about the priest and that there was a deep affection between the two men. However, the policeman didn't say anything, he just waited for the priest to go on.

"Andy had a paper he had been given by the lawyer. It was a written confession that, he said, they had compiled together, but I think it was written by the lawyer, because Andy would never have written anything like that. The lawyer is saying that the evidence against Andy is strong and that it will be difficult to prove his innocence. He told him that by declaring himself guilty, he would avoid a trial, be accused of second-degree murder and he would be granted extenuation. What worries me is that he is so confused that, in the beginning when I arrived, he even said he didn't remember clearly what happened. I made him talk and I succeeded in convincing him not to sign those papers and to tell the lawyer he prefers to face a trial than confess to a crime he didn't commit. I took the papers from him." He took them from the drawer of his desk and handed them to Jason, who took them and had a quick look at them. The priest went on, "But tomorrow, he will see the lawyer and I am afraid he will try to convince him once more. He said that even his wife has accepted what the lawyer is saying. This is the effect that a knowledgeable man like an attorney can have on a simple honest family. They are scared and the counsellor can convince them of what the best way is, but I don't think this is the only way. What do you think, Jason?"

"I am a little perplexed at the behaviour of this lawyer because he doesn't seem to consider Andy's innocence in the least. Andy talked to me the night of the murder, as I have told you, Mark, and his story was straight and he seemed sincere. You know that I can usually recognize a liar. Cooper was certainly frightened but seemed honest in what he was telling me. The problem is that, if he confesses, the case will be closed and I won't be able to investigate. I am looking into the life of Brown, the victim, who seemed to have some enemies and a lot of money problems and I have some people to talk to tomorrow who can be linked to Brown's death. I hope Cooper will follow your advice, but we have to talk to his family because I believe they are more scared than he is and they are not helping him." While he was talking, he turned to Maria, who was listening silently.

Now she said, "Yesterday evening, I called Meg and I said I would like to visit her and her mum this afternoon. She accepted eagerly but I heard her mum trying to invent an excuse to dissuade me. I told Meg that I didn't want to disturb them but she insisted, and finally, her mum accepted. I think they are very reserved people who are not used to talking about their problems with outsiders.

"Furthermore, they don't know me very well, I am just a foreigner from Meg's mum's point of view and I hope I will be able to gain her confidence. Thanks for sharing the information with me, I would like to have a look at the confession." Jason immediately handed it to her. "Perhaps, reading it together with Meg and her mum, I will be able to show them the absurdity of confessing to a crime you have not committed."

Father Mark looked at Maria with gratitude and said, "Thanks, Maria, I hope you will succeed in at least convincing them to wait. I am sure that if his wife realizes what is best, Andy will be more encouraged. His wife is a great support for him."

Jason gave Maria his business card and added, "Maria, if you don't mind, can you call me if you think Meg or her mum have told you something important?"

Maria took the little card and put it in her handbag, together with the confession papers. "Yes, I will certainly do so as soon as I finish my visit. I hope I will be able to help them. Thank you, Mark, for your trust."

Father Mark watched her as she went out of the room and he noticed that Jason watched her leave with what looked like admiration; he had seldom seen that look on his face, a mixture of sweetness and detachment. He knew that Jason did not easily give in to his emotions and his feelings, not since he had decided to remain alone.

"I think she is courageous, coming to a foreign country alone and facing a new experience by herself," Jason said as he turned his attention to the priest.

"Don't think that she has had an easy life, Jason. In fact, she has suffered a lot, even if a different type of sorrow from yours." Father Mark went on, talking more to himself than to Jason, "Everyone has his or her cross to carry, light or heavy, big or small. But she came here to start a new life and I think she is really a good teacher and she loves her job and her students."

Jason remained a few minutes longer, then he took his leave because he had some paperwork to do at his office and Father Mark had to take the Eucharist to some old and invalid people in the parish, as he did every Sunday.

Chapter 12

Sunday afternoon, September 21st

It was a pleasant late summer afternoon, the sun was shining but there was a slight breeze that made the temperature mild and enjoyable. Maria left home to drive the short distance to Meg's home. She was not completely familiar with her new car and with all the streets and routes of the town but she had studied the map on her mobile phone and she was fairly confident it would be easy to reach the quiet popular neighbourhood where Meg and her family lived. It was so different from Italy, where the popular quarters were mainly occupied by tall buildings and blocks of flats. Here, every family had their small house with a little garden in the front and a tiny space in the back too. In front of the house, there was generally a driveway for the car that led to the garage next to the main building. The houses were typically two-floor buildings and the gardens were tidy and neat, with beautiful flowers and plants that showed the love that every family had for their green space.

Maria parked in front of Meg's home and walked along the short path leading to the beautiful porch. She had not yet climbed the three steps that led to the front door when Meg came out and ran to embrace her teacher. In that welcoming hug, there was all the need for comfort and love that Meg felt, all the desperation and the worry visible in the troubled face of the young girl, who had dark bags under her eyes for want of sleep and rest. Maria affectionately hugged her young student and entered. Meg's mum stood in the little foyer which consisted of a coat hanger with a little table beneath it and a mirror on the wall. The home gave the impression of simplicity but of great care and tidiness. On the little table, there was a crocheted doily and a small vase with fresh flowers from the garden.

An arch led to the sitting-dining room which was not large but full of light from the big windows overlooking the garden. Beyond this room through a door, you could see the small but pristine kitchen, with wooden cabinets and cupboards and a small table next to the wall.

Meg's mum was much more reserved in her welcome, she simply took Maria's hand and said, "I am sorry Meg insisted so much on your coming today. You shouldn't have bothered." The tone of Mrs Cooper's voice was not encouraging but Maria had expected nothing less and she persisted.

"It's no bother at all, Mrs Cooper. I saw Meg so depressed and worried the other day that I came to see how you are both doing."

The woman was a little soothed by the calm and comforting tone of the teacher and she said more kindly,

"Come in, please! We can sit down in the living room. Would you like a cup of tea? I am sorry but we only have American coffee," she added with a tentative smile, hinting at Maria's origins.

"And I am sorry to say that I have not got used to your coffee yet," Maria said with a pleasant smile, "so a cup of tea will be OK for me, thanks. But first, let me tell you I don't want to intrude. Father Mark is worried about Mr Cooper and you, and I understand he has known your family for a long time and trusts your husband. I see him so preoccupied these days and he has asked for my help. I simply think that talking to a person who is outside your acquaintances would make you feel more at ease and maybe you could see things from a different point of view." Maria was afraid she was talking too much but she saw that Meg's mum was listening carefully to what she was saying and she was not giving any sign of discomfort or refusal. In the meantime, they had sat down; Maria on a sofa and mother and daughter on the other.

"Thanks, Miss Busati. My daughter has said wonderful things about your first Italian lessons, she is so enthusiastic about the Italian culture. We appreciate your concern but we have been advised by my husband's lawyer not to talk to people."

Meg reacted to these words and her voice was really anguished and full of fear. She was on the verge of tears but she spoke firmly, "This is what I can't accept, Mum. That lawyer is certainly an expert and knowledgeable but he doesn't know dad as we know him. Dad is not guilty, he has never done anything wrong. How can he believe that he killed someone? How can YOU believe it? I have tried to make myself think that this is the easiest way, that the evidence is strong and that in a trial he would never be able to prove his innocence, Miss Busati, but I can't, I can't..." her voice trailed off and she started to cry. Maria was deeply moved by this teenage girl who was defending her dad with all her might. This was what Maria would have done with her beloved dad.

Meg's mum embraced her daughter. "I know, love, it is difficult, but the lawyer said that it will be impossible to prove that dad didn't do it." Her voice was not as self-confident as it had been before. Maria understood that this was the time she could try to learn something more.

"But there must be someone else who wanted to kill Brown." Maria did not want to talk about her short conversation with Jason Grant.

"He says that there are other people who may have had the motive but only dad knew that Brown was in the office so late. He was not used to staying at work long hours," Meg said.

"And only my husband had the keys to enter the building," her mum added.

Maria asked, "Did you see Mr Brown sometimes? What do you know about him? Maybe even a comment from your dad about his colleague could be important."

Mother and daughter looked at each other and both thought the same thing; why had the lawyer not asked anything like that? Sure, that Detective had tried to ask them something of this kind, but Meg's mum had cut him off because they had just talked to Andy's attorney who had ordered them not to talk to the police. Meg and her mum started to see things from a different point of view. It was as if a kind of veil was being lifted and they could see things freely, without the filter of the lawyer's words.

Grace Cooper said, "Steve came sometimes to have lunch with us. He was so lonely even if he had so many friends, if you can call them that. They often called him while he was here but I remember they were not pleasant calls. The language was vulgar and my husband told me he had the habit of gambling and he was often in debt." Mrs Cooper stopped abruptly and seemed to remember something:

"Oh, my God, Meg, do you remember Brown came with a girl one day to introduce her to dad? When was it? Before you went back to school, a few weeks ago. She seemed a good girl, I think she is a hairdresser or something like that. What was her name? Julia… , no, her name is Jill. It was a pleasant evening but then Steve received one of those phone calls, and after that, he was so upset they had to leave. Jill was visibly worried and nervous. Maybe that girl knows something."

Maria was aware that Meg and her mum were starting to see things differently. Before she could say anything, Meg stood up all of a sudden and went to a drawer in the kitchen. She took a mobile phone and took it to her mum.

"Mum, do you remember that we found this mobile phone one day, two or three weeks ago, and we didn't know who it belonged to? Dad asked around in his office because he was convinced he had taken it and brought it home by mistake, but no one was looking for this mobile phone. And if it were that girl's? Maybe we could find her."

Maria took her bag and rummaged inside it in search of Jason's business card. Finally, she found it.

"Mrs Cooper, Meg, do you mind if we call Detective Grant now and tell him what you have just remembered? Maybe you can give him the cell phone." Maria had the impression that she had to take advantage of this moment because if Meg or her mum talked to that lawyer again, he could make them change their mind.

Mrs Cooper said, "I was not very kind to Detective Grant when he came to talk to us, but the lawyer insisted on our not speaking to the police and Mr Grant is so serious, so professional, he seemed to consider my husband guilty... I was kind of afraid of him..."

"This morning I met him after the mass and Father Mark introduced us." Maria wanted to justify her having his business card, "but I had the impression of a fair person and he said that when he talked to your husband, he seemed sincere to him."

"I don't know, he is always so detached, he seems indifferent and people say he is very tough. And he believed my husband was sincere before they found the money in the office. Andy says that certainly Mr Grant has now changed his mind about his innocence." Mrs Cooper sounded still a little afraid, "but I am worried because my husband told me that he is meeting his lawyer tomorrow. He told us that Father Mark has taken the confession the lawyer had prepared and now he doesn't know what to tell the counsellor when he meets him. He will certainly get angry. My husband is tired and depressed, poor man, and I wouldn't want him to sign the confession because now I am starting to see things differently."

"I have got the confession here with me." She took the papers out of her bag and put them on the coffee table in front of her. "Father Mark gave it to me this morning, but certainly the lawyer could write a new one. Excuse me, but we had better call Mr Grant!" She was careful not to call the detective by his first name.

She went out onto the porch, closed the door behind her and dialled Jason's phone number on her mobile phone. Jason answered almost immediately.

"Grant," he said in a professional tone.

"Hi, Jason, it's Maria." His voice became immediately very kind.

"Hi, Maria, any news?" Maria had difficulty hiding her excitement. She briefly put him up-to-date about what she had discovered, underlining the trust and confidence she had obtained and the fact that it could be only temporary, but Jason surprised her by saying that he would be there in a quarter of an hour, twenty minutes at the most.

"Can you wait for me there, Maria? I would like you to be present," he asked. "If you can, of course..." he added tentatively.

"Yes, sure, I will be here. Thanks, Jason!"

Jason arrived really soon, while Maria had been able to ease the tension by talking about her first impressions of Canada and her hometown. The tension started to increase again when the bell rang and Meg's mum went to let Detective Grant in.

Meg's mum said immediately, "Good evening, Mr Grant. I am sorry for having been rude a few days ago. I should have talked to you earlier." She cast her eyes down, embarrassed, but Jason said,

"Don't worry, Mrs Cooper, it's understandable under the circumstances. Miss Busati told me that you remember a girl who came with Brown and that you have a mobile phone that is not yours."

While he was speaking, he went into the living room and looked at Meg, who was beginning to cry once more. She was starting to sob softly with her face in her hands. He felt sympathy for that poor teenage girl. He sat next to her on the sofa and took her hand. Maria didn't expect this tender approach and she was really moved. Father Mark was right when he said that Jason was a good policeman but Maria started to see a sensitive man too.

"Meg, if your dad sees you crying, what will he think? Look at me, Meg, don't be afraid!" Meg slowly raised her eyes to look at Jason. "If your dad declared what is written in that confession," he pointed at the papers that were lying on the coffee table in front of him, "would it be better? He could avoid a trial but he would be in prison for some time. Why, Meg, if he is innocent? I am investigating and..." he smiled at her encouragingly, "I honestly don't believe he is guilty!" Hearing this, Meg gave a deep sigh of relief and it was visible that she was refraining from embracing the policeman.

"Thanks, Mr Grant," she said still looking at him. Her voice was full of gratitude and emotion, "this is what I have been telling mum. I believe my dad is innocent and I don't want him to pay for someone else's crime." She turned to her mother who was taken aback by the policeman's behaviour. "Don't you think, mum, that at least dad could wait for a few days before signing anything and see what happens with the investigation?"

Mrs Cooper had the troubled face of a person who is waking up from a nightmare. That lawyer surely meant well but he had conditioned her so much.

"Mr Grant, what shall we do now?" she asked as she was sitting next to Maria on the other sofa while Jason remained beside Meg. "I am afraid I have contributed to convince my husband that what the lawyer is saying is right and today I told him that he shouldn't have given the confession to Father Mark! Help us, please!" Her voice was pleading and Maria took her hand to try to comfort her but she understood the anguish of the poor woman.

Jason thought for a few minutes, then he took out his mobile phone and dialled a number. It was the prison and he asked for the time of the appointment of Cooper with his lawyer the following morning.

After he had ended the call he spoke, choosing his words carefully so as not to increase the tension of Cooper's wife and daughter.

"Tomorrow your husband has an appointment with the lawyer at ten a.m. Mrs Cooper, I think you should be there and ask to be present; it is your right and nobody can deny it. I think you should be there a little earlier, nine-thirty a.m. maybe and bring back the confession to your husband. Talk to him, explain what has just happened and that you have talked to me. When the lawyer arrives, be careful; your husband should not say that he doesn't want to sign, but just ask for a few days to think it over, OK?"

"But my husband will never sign a similar confession!" Meg's mum said while she was taking a look at the papers.

"Yes, I know, but I would like to see what that lawyer is going to do if he has to wait. There is something that doesn't convince me about that attorney. Trust me, and please, do as I have told you. Will you do this for me? Don't worry, your husband will not sign a false confession." Jason's voice was professional but he was very kind.

"Yes, Mr Grant. I will tell my husband what you have told me." Mrs Cooper was eager to help Andy now and she knew she could trust the detective. She had one important thing to ask, "If the lawyer asks whether I have talked to the police, what shall I say?"

"This is important, Mrs Cooper; don't say anything about our conversation, please." Meg's mum nodded and stood up.

"I wasn't very polite with you the day after my husband was arrested. I promised Miss Busati a cup of tea and I have not made it yet and I haven't offered you anything, Detective Grant."

Jason smiled and said, "Thanks, Mrs Cooper. I will have a cup of tea, please." In reality, he didn't want to stay much longer but he felt that it was important to gain the confidence of Mr Cooper's family. While they were having tea, Jason tried to turn on the mobile phone, but the battery was evidently dead, so he took it and said he would give it to the police technicians. Meg and her mum repeated what they had told Maria about the girl that had come with Brown which was not much.

After drinking tea and a few minutes of pleasant chat, Maria and Jason took their leave after revising with Mrs Cooper what she was to do and say the following day. Mrs Cooper promised to call Detective Grant after the visit to the prison to inform him and he gave her his business card. For the second time, Meg refrained from embracing the detective but she embraced Maria and thanked her warmly for her visit. Maria said simply,

"I am happy to see that you are feeling more confident and I am sure the detective will find the real murderer. Thanks for the tea, Mrs Cooper. I hope we will meet when all this is over. I will be glad to meet your husband."

Mrs Cooper shook the hand of Maria much more warmly than when she had arrived and expressed her gratitude.

Before they drove away, Jason called Father Mark to inform him about the developments. After the brief call, he turned to Maria and said:

"I know Father Mark is never wrong in judging people but he really was right when he said that you are wonderful at gaining the confidence of teenagers and their families," Jason said in a low voice. "Thanks for your help." Maria looked into the dark blue eyes of the detective and she believed she saw less sadness than before, a strange light in his gaze.

"I was happy to be able to help this family. I think they were really influenced by what the lawyer had told them and they couldn't see things clearly, maybe also with the shock of Cooper's arrest. And you were so kind to Meg, I believe that she and her mum have been influenced by what people say about your being a tough policeman, but I think they will trust you from now on and be a little less intimidated." Jason smiled and said,

"I know that people here in Trinity still consider me a stranger because I have been concentrated on my job and detached from the life of the community. But that poor girl is going through such a hard time." He looked at Maria and added, "I will call you tomorrow to bring you up to date about the situation if I'm not disturbing you!" Jason knew he sounded really shy, or maybe he was already trying to back down because he believed he had already gone too far in a relationship for his taste. Years before, he had vowed he would stay alone, he didn't want to cause suffering or put the life of a dear one in danger again.

"Call me whenever you want. My lessons end at three p.m. Then I will be at home! See you, Jason!"

Jason watched Maria as she drove away. Would he be able to be faithful to the promise he had made to himself? He knew that he had been particularly kind and soothing with Meg but when he saw a teenage girl he was always reminded of… He sighed and drove back to his office.

Chapter 13

Monday, September 22nd

When Jason arrived at the police station, Agent Hogan told him that Bill Tucker was waiting for him in the interrogation room. Jason gave Hogan the cell phone he had been given the day before and told him to hand it to the lab technicians, explaining briefly what he had learned at the Coopers'. The detective went into his office to take a folder he had prepared the day before and he took it with him.

Bill Tucker watched him enter. He was a short man in his late fifties with the face of a person no one would want to meet on a dark street at night. He had a perpetually arrogant expression of a person who is used to obtaining whatever he wants through menacing and violence. He had crew-cut grey hair, dark eyes and a goatee. He had an enormous tattoo visible on his left arm, depicting a terrible-looking snake. He was wearing stained jeans of a colour that could have been blue or grey and a checked white and red shirt with rolled-up sleeves.

Jason sat down opposite him and laid the folder on the table. "Hi, Tucker! Do you remember me?"

"Of course, Grant. I haven't seen you in quite a while though. I still don't know why I am here and I have already asked for a lawyer."

"You are not under arrest, Tucker, not yet at least," Jason answered calmly and continued, "When I decide to arrest you, you can call a lawyer, so don't get nervous. I am going to ask simple questions and I want straight answers from you, OK?"

"It depends on the questions, Detective!" Tucker said defiantly.

"Where were you last Thursday evening, say between eight and ten? This is a very simple question!"

"I won't answer if you don't tell me what's going on!"

Jason was absolutely indifferent to the tone of the answer, he opened the file and started to scan through the pages. Bill was watching him intently.

"Well, let's put it like this. Here I see a lot of things, let's say, a little beyond the limits of legality, that I could pin on you very easily. I could even close up that garage of yours. So I think you had better answer my questions." He looked straight at the man in front of him and went on, "Unless, of course, you have something to hide, much worse than what I can see here."

Bill pretended not to care about what Jason had said but there was a perceptible change in his expression and his demeanour.

"I insist on knowing what happened last Thursday!" he persisted, but a little less arrogantly.

"I ask questions here, Tucker, and YOU answer," the policeman said firmly. The tone, emphasized by Jason's hoarse voice and the slamming of his fist on the table, added to his annoyance and Bill understood that challenging Grant would not be the right choice. Being used to these situations, he knew when it was time to fight and when it was time to back up.

"OK, I don't remember exactly but I closed my garage at six p.m., you know I live just above the garage. Before I went home, I went to the bar opposite for a couple of beers, but I didn't stay long 'cause I was tired."

"You didn't go to the Trucker last Thursday night, did you?"

If Bill was surprised by the question, he did not show it. "No, I sometimes go there at the weekend to meet some friends, not on Thursday!"

"Was Steve Brown one of your FRIENDS?"

Jason was looking keenly at the man opposite him and he was checking for any reaction, big or small, as the questions were getting more direct and to the point. At Jason's mentioning Steve Brown, Tucker showed a slight expression of surprise which would have escaped a less experienced detective than Jason.

Anyway, he immediately recovered his composure and said, "Yes, we used to meet at the Trucker to play cards, if that's what you mean." He was trying to sound casual but Jason noticed that he was getting nervous.

"We know that he was often in debt with you, wasn't he? So I think it was more than a couple of card games."

"I know he was killed and you want to pin his murder on me but I have nothing to do with it. If he owed me money, why should I have murdered him? And every once in a while he paid his debts, so I can't complain!"

"How did he pay his debts? Where did the money come from?"

"I don't know! The only thing I know is that every two or three months he came to me with an envelope with money! I don't usually ask where the money comes from, as long as I am paid back."

"I think you have just said that you don't have an alibi for the night of the murder, am I right?" Jason changed the subject even if he was sure that Tucker knew much more than he let on.

"I don't need an alibi because I didn't do anything." Now Tucker was visibly nervous. "If you don't mind, I have a garage to manage and a lot of work to do!"

"Don't move out of town, Tucker, I will need to talk to you again in the next days."

Tucker had already stood up, and as soon as the door was opened, he immediately left. Jason remained for a few moments sitting at the table. He thought that Tucker was the most obvious suspect because of his past records and his relation to the victim, but there was still something that Jason couldn't grasp, there was something more to this murder.

As he came out of the interrogation room, he asked to talk to Hogan again. He asked the agent to have Tucker shadowed wherever he went and to report any movement to him.

***

Mrs Cooper left her husband, after talking to him and the lawyer. She was sad seeing her beloved man in prison, he was so dejected and depressed. They would celebrate their twentieth anniversary next month and they were planning on inviting her sister and family, his brother and wife, to have a pleasant day after the mass with the renewal of their wedding vows. She thought she had been really lucky to find Andy; he was a hardworking man, devoted to his family. When their daughter was born they were so happy and it had been wonderful to see her grow up into a sweet, sensitive child and then a wise, intelligent and generous teenage girl. Now their little peaceful world seemed to be coming apart and she hoped that Detective Grant had been sincere when he had told Meg that he believed Andy was innocent. It had done Meg so much good to talk to her teacher and the detective, and both had been so kind and considerate. She had heard a lot of talk about the tough homicide detective who had moved to Trinity, but yesterday, he had been really gentle, maybe because he knew what they were going through.

She took the phone from her purse and dialled the number written on Jason's business card. The detective answered after a few rings.

"Detective Grant. I am Grace Cooper, Andy Cooper's wife!"

The detective became immediately very kind and what surprised Grace was that he first asked how her husband was and not what was certainly more interesting for him.

"How is your husband, Mrs Cooper? Father Mark found him so sad yesterday and he is so worried."

Grace knew that the detective was a long-time friend of the priest but she noticed a great concern in Grant's words.

"He is still worried but I think he was relieved when I told him that I didn't want him to sign the confession. With the lawyer, we stuck to what you had recommended and we just asked for some more time to think about it. Mr Grant, it was the first time I had spoken to this attorney but I didn't like him. At first, he didn't want me to stay, but I said what you had told us about my right to be present and he didn't object, even if it was evident that he was not happy."

Jason was listening perplexed at what Mrs Cooper was telling him. He asked, "What was his reaction when you told him you wanted to wait?"

"I think at first he thought it was my idea and he asked Andy if it was his decision because he told him that nobody could decide for him. Mr Grant, that is what the lawyer has done up to now, he has decided for my husband!" Jason smiled at Grace's remark which was correct and to the point. He thought that knowledgeable men should beware of simple but sensible people like the Cooper family. "When Andy declared that he had thought about it and didn't want to sign so soon, the lawyer was visibly annoyed but he said we could wait 'a couple of days' (he used these words). At first, he said he would be back at the prison in two days, next Wednesday afternoon, but then he checked his mobile phone and changed it to Thursday afternoon because he said he had another appointment on Wednesday. Detective Grant, will it be enough? What shall we do then?" Her voice was pleading and anxious and Jason realized that the stress Andy and his family had suffered so far was becoming unbearable.

"Now, you don't have to worry, Mrs Cooper," he said soothingly, "if there is no important news or further developments by Thursday, we'll decide what to do, OK?"

"Oh, Detective Grant, I know you are doing everything you can, I know you are a good detective and Father Mark trusts you, but I am still worried because my husband can't sleep, and I see him wasting away in that prison." She was on the verge of tears and Jason said,

"Mrs Cooper, you have to be courageous now as you have been so far and encourage your husband. Go to visit him as often as you can and don't let him see that you are frightened." He paused and added, "and don't apologize to me, I understand what you are going through. You must trust me, Mrs Cooper!"

"I do, Mr Grant, WE do, Andy, Meg and I trust you and pray that you will find that criminal soon. Thanks, Detective!"

"I hope to be able to give you good news soon, Mrs Cooper, "bye for now!"

Grace ended the call and wondered why so many people said that Jason Grant was a hard cop. For her and Meg he had been a great help and comfort so far.

***

As soon as Bill Tucker was in his pick-up truck outside the police station, he took out his mobile phone and dialled a number. He was not as self-confident now as he had pretended to be in front of Grant.

After a few rings, the person he was calling answered.

"Hi, it's Bill. Why don't you answer on the other phone? Listen to me, I don't want to be mixed up in this murder. Why did the police want to talk to me? You told me that Cooper had confessed. What's the matter?"

He listened for a few minutes and his nervousness increased visibly, "What do you mean the secretary saw me talking to Brown and wants to go to the police? I don't have anything to do with this matter, but remember, if I am dragged down I will drag you down with me! You know what I mean!"

Again, he listened and answered, "Of course, I didn't say anything to the police but you know that Detective Grant, he is not one you can fool around as you like, he is clever! He has already gathered information about my business."

After listening again, he said, "Give me the address of that secretary."

The person on the other end spoke.

"OK, I don't know when I will be able to do something!"

He paused while the other person spoke.

"OK, don't get nervous, I will see what I can do." And he hung up with a curse.

***

Jason dialled Maria's phone number at four that afternoon, hoping she would be available. "Hi, Maria, it's Jason."

Maria's voice was not so cheerful and pleasant as the day before; she seemed distracted and sad. "Hi, Jason, how are you?"

"I am OK but… is this a bad moment? I don't want to disturb you!"

"I am sorry, Jason, it's not a bad moment and I am eager to learn if there is something new in the investigation. It's just that…" her voice trailed off. Could she talk about her unpleasant exchange of messages with her stepsister with a person she scarcely knew? Why did she, who had never talked about her problems to anyone, suddenly feel the urge to talk to a person she hardly knew? Maybe because she missed her dad and she felt she needed someone near her so she said, "I am at home now. Maybe I am asking too much, but I don't like to talk on the phone about important things like the Coopers' situation. Would you mind coming here for a cup of coffee or tea? We can talk more comfortably."

Jason understood that Maria had something that weighed on her heart; was he overstepping the boundaries he had put on himself if he went to her? He listened to his heart.

"I don't like talking on the phone either. If you give me your address I can be there, let's see… Do you mind if I come after dinner? Would eight be too late for you?" Maria accepted and gave him her address.

When she hung up she felt strangely relieved. When she had a problem, she was used to talking to her dad and he always found the right words to say to her, but now she missed him so much. She clutched her father's wedding ring in her hand and tears rolled down her cheeks. 'Will this nastiness ever stop? What does my sister still want from me?'

She stood up and went to her desk to correct some homework and she promised herself not to tell Jason anything about her past, not for the time-being, at least.

When she had finished correcting her students' work, she took her laptop and wrote to Father Giulio. She had so much to tell him this week.

'Dear Giulio, thanks for the unfailing mail. Yesterday I wanted to answer you immediately but there was also an email from my stepsister, Raffaella, that disturbed me. She asked me if I have taken a gold pen that belonged to my dad and that she remembered it was in one of the boxes I

prepared before we sold the apartment. She said that she wanted it and that I have to give it back. Giulio, why is she always so nasty to me? I perceive this as a great injustice because I have never done anything less than kind to her, you know that the more she treated me with disregard the more I did everything I could to gain her affection. But now, I didn't take that pen, I assure you. I don't know if I have to answer and I know that, whatever I tell her, she will remain convinced that I have taken it.

But I have to tell you about what happened last week. The dad of one of my students, one of my best students, has been accused of the murder of one of his colleagues. Father Mark is convinced that he is innocent, he knows the suspect, Mr Andy Cooper, very well because he is one of his most helpful parishioners. Father Mark introduced me to the detective in charge of the investigation, Jason Grant, who is a very kind man, but you can see clearly that he is suffering for something. They asked me to talk to the family of the suspect; a wonderful united family. I went to visit them yesterday. Meg, my student and her mum are worried and scared. Pray, Giulio, for a fast positive solution to this investigation because too many people are suffering. Meg's best friend, Louise, is the daughter of the manager of the company where the employee was killed and where Meg's dad works. Yesterday, after the mass she asked to talk to me, but today she was not at my lesson. I will wait until Wednesday when I have another class with her, and I hope I will be able to talk to that girl because she seemed as frightened and worried as her friend.

My job here is continuing satisfactorily. I am happy I have decided to accept this experience and I will never be able to thank you enough for offering it to me, Giulio. Pray for me and give me your advice about what to write to Raffaella.

Love, Maria'

***

Alison Lewis finished work a little later, at five-forty-five that afternoon. She stopped at the supermarket to do some food shopping and arrived home at about six-thirty p.m. Today at work it had been a little quieter than last Friday and Mr Kilton was decidedly less nervous. When she told him that she had seen Brown put the envelopes into Cooper's drawer and talk to a strange man in the hall and the parking lot, he had seemed indifferent and not particularly concerned, but in the meantime, one of the salesmen, who often talked to Brown, had entered and she suspected he had heard something. Nevertheless, the manager cut her off immediately. He remarked that they could have been different envelopes or that he could have found them in the drawer and put them back. But she was sure they were the right ones and that she was not mistaken. Anyway, the manager had told her that, if she felt it was her duty, she should certainly go to the police but he had said he had never heard of a person named Bill. Then, during lunch break, Kilton had asked her to prepare some important papers and she didn't have enough time to go to the police station.

Now it was too late but she thought that tomorrow she could go there during lunch break. Now that she had made up her mind, she was more serene, maybe it was just as Kilton said that what she had seen had nothing to do with the murder. She was so sad thinking of Andy in prison as he was the kindest person on earth, who frequently asked her about her mother, always saw when she was sad, and most of all, she was sure he was not a killer.

When she arrived home, she prepared dinner then she settled on her sofa to watch TV as she did every night. She particularly liked reality shows, those new television series about home makeovers. The events of the last days had left her sad and fatigued. She couldn't help thinking of that poor Steve Brown, so lonely and so kind to everyone and of Andy, who was really one of the most honest and polite people she had ever met.

She turned on the TV and she was watching it with interest when the doorbell rang. Nobody ever came to her after dinner, who could it be?

She slowly stood up and went to the door. She distractedly opened it a bit to see who it was and she felt a hand grabbing the door and opening it. Instinctively, she backed off toward the little table where she kept her phone, but that dark shadow grabbed her and held something above her head... then a sharp blow and... darkness!

***

The man in the dark car was really nervous. Nothing was going as he had predicted or expected. And now that woman, that secretary was complicating things even more. If she went to the police, maybe it wouldn't change anything because she had just seen Brown put the envelopes in the drawer, but certainly, they would investigate, and that Detective seemed smart and was known for being one who never gave up until he reached the truth.

And then there was Andy Cooper who still had not signed a confession. If he had signed, everything would be clear and nobody would look for other suspects.

And now, after shadowing the secretary from the office to her home to make sure she didn't go to the police, he was waiting to see if someone else would do the dirty job instead of him but he didn't trust that crook.

He waited not far from Alison Lewis's home where he was not seen but could see who came and went. Her neighbour drove away at seven-fifteen and nobody came. Now it was almost eight p.m. and that crook hadn't come. The man began to fear the neighbour would come back. If he wanted to do something, he had to do it fast.

He got out of his car, he was wearing gloves, he took a wrench and went to Alison's door.

It is true that, once you start in the way of crime and murder, it is difficult to stop. The first time with Brown he had felt shame and remorse for a few minutes, now it was much easier. He just hit that woman with the wrench, opened drawers and cabinets, knocked a few chairs over to give the idea of a robbery and left, leaving the door open, being careful not to be seen by anybody. He didn't feel anything, just relief at another danger removed. Would there be another one on the way?

***

Jason was feeling strangely excited while he was driving to Maria's. 'Be careful,' he thought, 'you mustn't get involved, no more people you care for should suffer or die, as has already happened. Maria is better if she remains far from you.' That is what he had promised himself six years before after his personal tragedy. He was still feeling remorse because it was his job that had led to the death of his dear... He smiled, thinking that maybe he was just running too fast, maybe Maria was not interested in him. She was so sensitive, so kind but she had barely spoken to him, just a few words of courtesy. But today she had sounded so sad, so lonely, perhaps because, after all, she had been far from Italy for just a few weeks, maybe she was just feeling homesick.

He parked in front of Maria's little bungalow and walked the short path that led to the front door. He rang the bell and Maria opened almost immediately. She was wearing a light grey jumpsuit and her hair was gathered in a ponytail. She was not smiling as he had seen her when they had first met; she had a troubled expression on her face that was difficult not to notice, being so different from her usual jovial countenance.

"Thanks, Jason, for coming. Please, come in!" she simply said.

Jason entered and noticed a tiny home that was kept with great tidiness and taste.

"Maria, I don't want to intrude, I hardly know you, but you look tired and sad today. Is it a bad moment? Tell me, we can meet tomorrow if it's better for you." Jason was looking at her face with genuine apprehension.

Maria had a lump in her throat and could not answer, she just walked to the sofa and invited Jason to sit down. She sat on the armchair next to him and bent her face because she didn't want him to see the sadness in her eyes.

"Jason, don't worry!" she said after a few moments when she felt she could speak with a firm voice. "I have received some nasty messages from Italy from… a relative, so to speak, and I am always sad when this person treats me like this, but now I am ready to listen to the development in Andy Cooper's case. Would you like an Italian coffee?" she asked with a smile, standing up. "I have brought my moka with me from Italy."

"Thank you, Maria, I would like to try Italian coffee, but don't worry, I can sit at the table if it's more convenient for you!" The justification by Maria had not completely convinced him but he didn't want to insist. He followed her to the kitchen corner and dining area where the table was. He sat down on a chair while she was busy with the coffee. She took two cups from the cupboard and put them on the perfectly clean table, together with a beautiful glass sugar bowl.

Maria knew that her sad and off-putting welcome had discouraged Jason and she asked, "Have you discovered anything about the mobile phone that Meg found in her home?"

"Yes, it is a prepaid phone. I don't know if you have these kind of phones in Italy, but here in Canada, a person can buy a phone with prepaid credit and a provisional number, when they don't want to use their phone. Various phone calls had been made and we are checking the numbers. So far, we haven't discovered anything interesting, but some numbers have gone to voicemail and we are checking who they belong to. Mrs Cooper called me this morning to say that they have been able to convince the lawyer to wait for a few days, until Thursday afternoon. I hope it will be enough because Mrs Cooper still sounded worried and frightened." Jason noticed that Maria, after pouring coffee into the two cups, had gone to the window and was looking out. Jason stood and went towards her. She was looking so lonely, so sad, and she had been immediately so generous with her students, so concerned about their problems. Someone should take care of her, her family was so far away, 'if she had a family,' Jason thought.

"Maria," he said as she turned to look at him, "I know that we have met only once, but if there is something wrong and I can do something for you, you can come to me, you know!" he said tentatively.

Maria went back to the table and they sat down again. She looked embarrassed. "I am so ashamed, Jason. We are talking about the destiny of an innocent person, Andy Cooper, and I keep thinking about a stupid misunderstanding with a person who lives thousands of miles away and who has nothing to do with my life now. The fact is that sometimes you would like to know why certain people seem to enjoy tormenting you when you have done nothing to deserve it." She knew that Jason could not understand the meaning of what she was saying, because he knew nothing of her past and she was debating with herself whether to tell him or not when the detective's mobile phone rang. Jason excused himself and answered. From his sentences and the look on his face, Maria could tell that it was not good news.

When he ended the call, Jason said, "I am really sorry, Maria, but there has just been an attempted murder that can be connected to Cooper's case." Maria's eyes widened and she looked concerned.

"Attempted murder? Oh, my God. Who is it this time?"

"The secretary of Kilton Motor Company, Alison Lewis!" Jason did not regret telling Maria because he knew she was very reserved. "They have taken her to hospital, let's hope that they will be in time to save her life!"

He added apologetically, "I am sorry, Maria, but I have to go now." He was really sorry to leave her so sad and troubled.

Maria immediately said, "Of course, Jason, don't worry, I am OK and I hope that lady will recover soon and you will arrest that killer before he hurts anyone else!"

Jason left, and while he was driving to Alison Lewis's home, he kept thinking of that pleasant young woman he was starting to care about. 'No, Jason,' he said to himself, 'stay away from her. Don't make her suffer.'

Chapter 14

Tuesday, September 23rd

As soon as Jason woke up the following morning after a few hours of sleep, his first thought was for that poor woman who had been attacked in her home with a wrench. It was obvious she didn't intend to go anywhere and she didn't expect anyone because she was wearing her nightgown. When he arrived at her home, she had been taken to the hospital unconscious and they said she had suffered a severe concussion but she was still breathing, even if she had lost a lot of blood. Luckily, Gisela, her neighbour, had noticed her door ajar when she was coming home and she had immediately alerted the police.

When he had looked around her little house, he had seen chairs overturned and drawers opened and emptied, a lot of their contents scattered on the floor, but he was not convinced it was a burglary. Alison's handbag was still on her bed in her bedroom, the money had not been touched, and in one of the drawers, there was a little box containing a few jewels, but it had not been opened.

On the table in the kitchen, he had seen the mail she had opened that evening and he had noticed a bill coming from a nursing home. He had instinctively taken the bill and now he called the nursing home number.

The person who answered said that Alison Lewis's mother had been there for almost a year and that the next payment was due in a few days.

Jason knew how hard it was for a person who had to take care of a sick relative because the expenses were huge. He called the hospital where Alison had been taken the day before and they told him that she was still unconscious. She had undergone an operation to reduce the hematoma and now she was stable, but they couldn't say yet if she would survive or not.

Jason took the bill, and before going to the police station, he went to the bank to pay. If that poor lady didn't recover, her mum would be provided for at least a few months, if she recovered she would pay him back. Jason never thought about these things, it just came naturally to him to help a person if he could. He had lost his parents so soon, but at least he had not seen them suffer, he had not been obliged to assist them in their old age or a disease.

Knowing that Alison Lewis lived alone in the town and did not have any relatives, Jason next called Father Mark and asked him if he could go to the hospital to visit her so that she could have someone near. Father Mark agreed immediately, even if he had rarely seen her in church. The priest asked him what he thought about the aggression. Jason said it was too early to say. Then, without thinking, Jason asked, "Have you seen Maria today? I heard from her yesterday to inform her about the

Coopers but she seemed to have a problem with a relative in Italy." He didn't say he had actually gone to her home. "Unfortunately, we were interrupted because I received the call about the aggression…" his voice trailed off because he realized he had already spoken too much. Had he shown more interest in the Italian teacher than he wanted to?

Father Mark didn't seem to notice and just said, "As I have already told you, Jason, Maria has had her share of suffering. You know I don't like to talk about the personal situation of a person. If she feels like it, she will talk about it herself. I can only tell you that she is very lonely and she has not left a loving and affectionate family in Italy."

"I am sorry. Yesterday she was really sad! Anyway, I will get in touch with you when I learn something new, Mark! Have a nice day and thanks for your help!"

When Father Mark ended the call, he couldn't help but smile. Was Jason finally coming to terms with his tragedy and his isolation? Was God in His infinite mercy guiding him to serenity after so many years of remorse?

***

At the police station, Jason was told that Bill Tucker had been brought in once again for questioning. Agent Hogan informed Jason that the gangster had been shadowed continually since the detective had ordered them to do it and that, the previous night, they were absolutely certain he had not left his home. He was in the interrogation room but this time he was visibly nervous.

"Hi, Tucker!" Jason said

"Listen, Grant, I am getting tired of being brought here for no reason at all! I refuse to talk to you!"

Jason sat down opposite him and looked at him intently. He knew for certain that he was not responsible for the aggression last night, but he could have easily sent someone else to do the dirty job while he was fooling the police. No, there was something else connected to this story and the two attacks, something that was worth killing, something, Jason was sure, connected to money.

"YOU listen, Tucker. I know you have some connection with the Kilton Motor Dealer Company, I don't know yet with whom and what sort of connection you have, but I will soon find out. In your place, I would try to be a little more cooperative because, in that case, we could turn a blind eye to some of your so-called dealings. Think about it, Tucker." Jason leaned closer to Tucker's face and repeated, "Think about it!"

"I don't know anything about the Kilton company. I only knew Brown, as I have already said." But the more he declared this, the less Detective Grant believed it. Now he knew that this man had something to hide.

He opened a door and called Hogan, "Please, David, go with Tucker back to his garage and take all the documents you find there; all the account books, all the invoices, all the records you find, all the names of his customers, the phone books, all the contacts, everything!"

He deliberately sounded authoritarian but not for Hogan's benefit, just to show Tucker that he would go to the bottom of it all!

Tucker got up, looked at Grant defiantly and left with Hogan, without saying another word. Jason wanted to go to the Kilton company, but before he left, a young agent knocked on his office door.

He said, "Come in!"

The young agent looked at him reverently and said, "Excuse me, sir, but we have finally been able to reach one of the contacts on that prepaid phone you gave us yesterday!" Jason stopped what he was doing, immediately interested in what the young policeman was saying.

"A woman answered, her name is Jill Bennet, she became very nervous when she heard it was the police, but when we talked about Brown, she started to cry. She said she had never shown up because she didn't want to be involved, she lives in Oshawa and she works there. She said she can come to talk to us tomorrow if it is necessary."

"Oshawa, isn't it the town where Kilton attended the convention of car dealers the night of Brown's murder?" Grant looked at some papers on his desk. "Yes, it's the same place! OK, call her back and tell her to give you her address. I will talk to her tomorrow because I want to go to Oshawa anyway. Let me know what she tells you."

Jason waited while the agent made the phone call. He soon came back to tell him that she had given him her address and said she would be at home during lunch break because she worked in a hairdresser salon near her home.

"OK," Jason said, "tell her I will be there at about twelve-thirty p.m. Thanks!"

***

Father Mark met Maria in the corridor and he immediately saw that her drawn face betrayed her concern for something. She tried to just say 'hello' to him but he stopped her and said, "Maria," he didn't want to relate what Jason had told him, "I see that you look tired and sad today. You know you can always talk to me whenever you have something on your mind, don't you?"

Maria realized at that moment how lonely she was feeling, how desperately she missed her dad and how much the lack of real family bonds weighed on her. She would have liked to be able to reassure Father Mark that there was nothing wrong but her eyes filled with tears and she was only able to say,

"If you have a minute for me, Mark, I would be grateful."

Father Mark, without another word, led her to his study and closed the door behind her. He invited her to sit down in the same armchair where she had sat a few days before with Jason.

"What's the matter, Maria? Father Giulio told me something about your dad and about the fact that you just recently learned that you were adopted at birth. Has this sadness something to do with it?"

Maria gave a deep sigh! She needed so much to talk to someone. She instinctively clutched her dad's wedding ring hanging on a chain around her neck.

"I am so sorry, Mark. You have so many things to do and to think about, but after my father's death, I was so busy getting ready to come here and so excited about my new experience that I only seldom stopped to think about my loneliness. In reality, the only family I have ever had was my dad, he was the only one who cared for me, and when my mother died, we were so close, we talked about everything in harmony and we shared so many happy moments. My stepmother and my stepsister never accepted me and just yesterday my stepsister, Raffaella, sent me an email saying that she is looking for a gold pen my dad had and she can't find it. It's a stupid thing, but oh, Mark, if you read that email, the nasty words she uses saying that I have certainly taken it! I have kept nothing of my dad except his wedding ring." She showed the gold chain to Father Mark. "He gave me his wedding ring a few days before he died but I never took that pen! Yesterday I wrote an email to Father Giulio, as I do every week and I told him what had happened. This morning I read his reply. My dad gave his gold pen to Father Giulio a few weeks before he died because he wanted his dear friend to have something of his. Giulio told me that he is going to speak to Raffaella and he recommended not to answer that email and not to give my phone number here. I don't expect

Raffaella to apologize to me but why does she always use that scornful tone with me? Why never, never a kind word of, I don't say affection, but at least respect?" She realized that her voice was becoming anguished and that tears were rolling down her cheeks.

Father Mark had listened silently to her outburst. Now he came near her, he sat down in the other armchair and he took her hand.

"Maria, you are not alone now. You have your colleagues, your students who adore you and me, of course." He wanted to say that Jason was worried too but he preferred not to mention him.

Maria made a small smile and tried to sound a little more serene when she answered, "I know, Mark, I am happy here and I think I am doing a good job. But I can't avoid feeling a great void behind me, a wickedness I don't think I have deserved. After all, I have taken care of my dad to the end, while my sister only seldom visited him. I don't want to be thanked but at least to be respected. I know, Mark, we must never ask for gratitude and I am happy to have stayed near my dad even when he was ill and weak, but..." her voice trailed off.

"Gratitude, Maria, can be expressed in many ways. Your dad expressed his gratitude by making you feel loved. It is not necessary to say "Thanks" but a smile and a kind word can say much more, and you are right, you would have deserved at least a gentle word. But I think that, in the end, a person who writes a nasty email for a pen must be really unhappy and unfulfilled. I believe that, in the end, the lonely person is your stepsister, not you!"

Maria felt really comforted by Mark's words. "Thank you, Mark!" she said sincerely. "But… do you know anything about that woman who was attacked last night? Jason had come to me to talk about Andy Cooper's situation and they called him!" Father Mark instinctively smiled, 'Jason,' he thought, 'so you were at Maria's yesterday, a loner like you who never visits anyone? Well, well, this is a step forward.' He didn't show any surprise to Maria, though, and he said, "Jason called me this morning to tell me that she is alive and stable but she is alone here in town so I am going to visit her later today! Have you talked to Louise Kilton, by the way?"

"No, Mark, yesterday she was not in class. I hope to see her tomorrow!"

Father Mark was worried for Louise too, because he knew that she had a family that was not affectionate and supportive. He just said he hoped Maria could understand what troubled Louise so much. He said some more words of encouragement to Maria and she left, feeling much more comforted and less lonely than before.

***

Jason arrived at the Kilton company in the late afternoon. He went immediately to the first floor and knocked on Kilton's office door. Kilton opened the door personally and he couldn't avoid a surprised reaction at the sight of the detective.

"Oh, hi, Detective, I don't think you have called to announce your visit!" he said, not trying to conceal his annoyance. He was nervous, but Jason thought, this was understandable as one employee was dead, one employee was in prison and his personal secretary had been attacked.

"No, actually I didn't call. But I won't keep you, just a few questions and I will be on my way!" Jason tried to sound pleasant but Kilton's attitude irritated him; he didn't know why.

"OK, I have just a few minutes!" was the curt answer and Kilton moved to the armchair behind his desk without inviting the detective to sit down. Jason sat in the armchair opposite Kilton and went directly to the point.

"Do you know anything about the possible reason for your secretary's attack last night?"

"I don't know anything about the life of my employees or what they do when they are at home. I don't even know where they live. This is my policy, Detective, I am just a manager and I am not their friend or their confidant." 'The tone was really as cold and detached as his policy,' Jason thought.

"But she worked for you and with you, Mr Kilton. Did she look nervous yesterday? Did she say anything that could hint at a problem or a concern she had?"

Was Jason mistaken, or Kilton hesitated before answering? But it was only a matter of a few seconds, then he said in his scornful and self-confident tone, "No, I didn't notice anything in particular... Miss Lewis was often nervous, but I think it was part of her personality, so I didn't bother!"

Jason noticed that Kilton had not asked how Miss Lewis was and when he had talked to the hospital nurse, she had said that nobody had called to ask about her.

Now he said, just to see his reaction, "I really hope that Miss Lewis will recover. At the hospital, they told me that her condition is improving."

Kilton's reaction was upsetting: "Really? I thought she had very little hope of surviving!" Either Kilton was really insensitive or... Jason started to look at this cold, detached man in a different way.

He quickly took leave, went down the stairs and towards the exit of the car showroom that was on the ground floor.

At the reception, the girl he had talked to the day after Brown's murder, was waiting for him. She stopped him and he read her name on the tag, Carol Stevenson.

"Excuse me, Detective, can I talk to you a minute?" she was agitated and she kept looking towards the staircase, maybe afraid to see Kilton coming down.

"Yes, of course," Jason said kindly. She led him to the small office behind the reception and carefully closed the door.

"I have only a few minutes because I cannot leave the reception unattended," she said, "But Alison was such a sweet woman and that man," she pointed to the first floor "always scolded her and treated her as if she were stupid. I don't know why she didn't look for a better job.

Yesterday she told me that today during lunch break she intended to come to the police to talk about something she had seen or heard, I don't know, she did not explain further, but I think it had taken her some time to make up her mind and she seemed relieved! She added that she owed this to Andy who was always kind to her!"

"Thanks, Miss Stevenson. Do you know if she had talked about this with Mr Kilton?"

"She didn't mention it, I am sorry!"

Jason went away perplexed by what he had heard and he made up his mind about what to do next.

***

Louise was deeply saddened when she heard about the attack on her dad's secretary, but at the same time, she thought that now Meg's father would certainly be released because he could not be considered responsible for this crime since he was in prison. Maybe, after all, she wouldn't need to tell what she had seen that night and she wouldn't have to talk to her dad about the mobile phone she had hidden in a drawer in her bedroom. Maybe her dad would allow her to go back to school. He had been so angry with her in the past few days.

For the first time since last Thursday, she picked up her phone to call her friend, Meg, "Hi, Meg, how are you?"

"Hi, Louise, it's good to hear you. Yes, I am fine but I am so worried about my dad. He is still in prison."

"But Meg, now that another person has been attacked maybe they will reconsider the case and they will find the person who is responsible for both crimes!"

"I don't know, Louise. I don't think my dad's situation will change so much because the evidence against him in connection to Brown's murder is still strong. He was found there when the police arrived and they found money in his office drawer. Oh, Louise, your dad has been so kind to send him a lawyer, and certainly, the attorney means well but he is trying to convince him to declare himself guilty."

"No!" Louise interrupted her friend with an anguished voice. "He shouldn't do that!"

"But what can he do, Louise? If only someone had seen something that night."

Louise felt tears rolling down her cheeks. "Don't worry, Meg. Your dad is certainly innocent and the police will find the truth!"

"Thanks, Louise, tomorrow I will be at school, I hope to see you! I need your support so much now!"

"Certainly, Meg, I will be there! Have a good night!"

Louise ended the call before Meg could realize she was as frightened as her friend. Still upset, she turned her head and… at her bedroom door, her dad was standing with an angry scowl. He had listened to the conversation and he was looking at his daughter with a disapproving and even menacing expression on his face. Louise was really frightened now, she had never seen her dad look at her like this. She prayed he would not look for that mobile phone in her bedroom!

Chapter 15

Wednesday, September 24th

It was like a puzzle and Jason felt he needed some more pieces to fill the last empty spaces. Before leaving for the police station he called the hospital and they informed him that Alison Lewis had spent a quiet night and now there were some slight signs of improvement. He was glad to hear that and he asked the nurse to call him as soon as Miss Lewis would be able to talk to him.

Then he went to the police station but he stopped for just a few minutes to let Agent Hogan know that he would be in Oshawa to talk to the organizers of the convention where Mr Kilton was the night of the murder and then to talk to Jill Bennet. He always said where he was going, in case someone needed him.

He left in his car, still thinking about the case. The thing he had to clear up was the connection between Tucker and Kilton, if there was a connection.

His thoughts drifted to Maria, to that evening when she was so sad. At the thought of that young woman, so generous and at the same time so fragile, he felt a wave of tenderness but he reproached himself for going to her. He shouldn't have, he had to keep her at a distance no matter how much it would cost him, because he had promised himself not to get involved, not to have relationships that his job could put in danger. Better alone than sorry and remorseful, as he was feeling now, that was what he had kept repeating since Monday night, but oh, it was difficult because Maria was really an intelligent, sensitive woman, a woman who could understand him and his feelings... and he could not deny that he often thought of her and had started to feel something for her. No, too much suffering, too much remorse! Maybe in a few months, maybe later, when that criminal, that bastard, would be finally caught.

He arrived at the site of the convention in Oshawa and he asked to talk to the organizers. They introduced him to Mr Martin.

"Hello, Detective Grant!" the man said and led him to his office where he invited him to sit down. "I have already talked to an agent who asked me whether Mr Brian Kilton was here last Thursday at the convention!"

"Yes, I know," answered Jason, "but I wanted to know whether a person could come and go from the convention at will."

"In other words, Mr Grant, you are asking me if I can be sure that Mr Kilton was here from the beginning of the convention at six p.m. to the closing time at around nine-thirty p.m. Am I wrong?"

"No," said Jason smiling, "you are not wrong, that is exactly what I am asking you!"

"OK, let me see," Mr Martin picked up a folder from his desk and consulted the program of the convention once again. " From six to seven-thirty p.m. we had informative meetings about cars and the situation of car sales in Canada with experts and Mr Kilton was certainly present because he signed his admission into the lecture hall. After seven-thirty p.m. the car dealers just looked around the showrooms and talked to each other, and in this time lapse, it is really difficult for anyone to say whether a person went somewhere else. At closing time, at nine-thirty p.m., Kilton was certainly here because he spoke to me while we were leaving."

"Thanks, Mr Martin, you were very precise. So, no one can say that Kilton was here between seven-thirty p.m., and let's say, around nine-fifteen p.m., am I right?"

"Yes, that's right. I am sorry but the agent just asked me if Mr Kilton was at the convention and not if we can be sure he was here from the beginning to the end."

"Don't worry," said Jason, "thanks for your help, Mr Martin, I will need a list of the participants in the convention."

"I will print it out for you if you wait a minute." He went to the computer on his desk, and after a few minutes, the printer on the little table in the corner started to work. Mr Martin took four sheets of paper and handed them to Jason.

"Thanks, Mr Martin. Have a nice day!"

With these words, Jason left. One piece of the puzzle had been found and fit perfectly in the pattern.

***

Jill Bennet was a good-looking woman in her thirties, with soft, long, blond hair, brown eyes and a heavily made-up face. She was tall, of medium build and she had a sweet smile that made her more attractive. She was decidedly agitated that morning at work in the hairdresser salon, even if she tried not to show her nervousness to her clients or her boss. She looked forward to meeting that Detective, she didn't remember the name the agent on the phone had told her, but at the same time, she was afraid. Wouldn't it have been better for her to just say she didn't know Steve so well and leave it at that?

But Steve was a good man, he had been so kind to her, he really wanted to make her happy, and since the police had found her number (she didn't know how or where!), she just had to say what she knew. Maybe the investigators had already found out what she was going to tell them, maybe it was not so important, but she simply felt she had to talk to someone.

At noon she went to the bar opposite the salon to eat something, even if she was not hungry at all. Then she went back home to wait for the detective.

Detective Grant was famous for his punctuality and he arrived at precisely twelve-thirty p.m. He rang the bell and the young woman let him in. His aspect of seeming like a severe policeman didn't at first help to make her feel at ease, but then she reflected that she had nothing to hide, hadn't done anything wrong, had just fallen in love, or just been attracted to a man who was so courteous and kind, but unfortunately, was weak and hadn't been able, despite all his promises, to change his life and his habits.

When they were sitting in the tiny living room, Jason began, "Thanks, Miss Bennet, for agreeing to talk to me," he said in a kind tone because he perceived that the young woman was nervous. "How long had you known Mr Brown?"

The woman's eyes filled with tears at the name of Steve, but she recovered before answering in a firm voice, which, nevertheless, betrayed her emotion, "We had been seeing each other for a few months. We met for the first time last May. Then he contacted me after a few days and we started to go out together. We just went to the cinema or to walk at the lake, and once or twice, we went to Toronto. He started to talk about himself and I noticed that he had some habits I didn't like, he received phone calls that left him upset, once, I even overheard some menacing calls. I started to be afraid and I asked him to stop meeting those kind of people. I even threatened to leave him if he didn't change his life. Once, I even went to that Trucker diner, that horrible place, to stop him before he entered because I knew that that was the place where he lost a lot of money, but he didn't listen to me, or maybe he didn't want me to stay with those people, he wanted to protect me."

"Did he mention any name in particular? Did he say anything about who was menacing him?" Jason asked.

"He was afraid of someone. I can't remember his name."

"Was the name Bill Tucker, by any chance?"

"That was one of the names of the people who called him, but one day, he was really frightened and also sad because his boss had asked him to do something he didn't want to do. Something that involved that workmate of his, he introduced me to him... Andy, the man you arrested!"

"Was the boss a man named Kilton?"

"Yes, that's the name. He was more afraid of him than of the other bad guys who used to call him. Maybe because he was his boss and he had done something wrong, I don't know. But that colleague, Andy, was such a good person, I can't believe he could be mixed up in anything dishonest. Oh, I am sorry but I can't tell you anything more. I was trying to convince him to change his way of living, but I believe that it was too difficult. Oh, I am so sorry for Steve because, you see, he was a good man, he just had met the wrong people and he didn't know how to make things right..." her voice trailed off while she tried to look away so as not to show the detective that tears were coming to her eyes.

Jason said calmly and gently, "Miss Bennet, what happened was not your fault, I can assure you. You were very kind to talk to me today and you have helped me a lot, you know! I am sorry you lost your boyfriend, but believe me, you did everything you could to save him."

He stood up and put a hand on Jill's shoulder. "Thanks again, Miss Bennet, we hope to be able to arrest the murderer soon!"

She stood up and her fear of the detective had partially disappeared now, she felt she had done the right thing by talking to the police and she felt relieved.

"Thanks, Detective, you have been very kind."

Jason left and drove back to Trinity. Another piece of the puzzle but still many questions to answer.

***

Maria was happy when she noticed that Meg was present at her lesson, even if she still saw concern and strain on her face. It was apparent that she was doing her best to follow her teacher's explanation, but when she distractedly looked out of the window, Maria could feel she was thinking of her dad. Meg was lucky because her schoolmates were very kind-hearted and certainly they were trying to support her. In fact, this was Maria's best class, both for the results and for the atmosphere, which made lessons so pleasant and profitable. It was a pleasure to teach these young teenagers who were so eager to learn and so interested in the Italian language and culture.

On the other hand, Maria was dismayed when she saw that Louise was not in class. She had asked to talk to her after the lesson. What could have happened to her? She was Kilton's daughter, Maria reflected and she imagined the stress she had gone through in the last few days, with a murder, an aggression in her dad's company, and further, her best friend's father in prison.

When the lesson finished, Meg approached her. Her face was still very pale but she was doing her best to smile.

"Meg, how are you and your mum?" Maria asked while she was putting her books in her bag.

"We are fine, Miss Busati, but now I am worried about Louise too. She told me yesterday that she would be in class today, but when I saw this morning she was not at the Maths lesson, I called her. She sounded really strange. She told me she was not feeling well and that she would not come for a few days. I sensed she wanted to tell me something more but she abruptly stopped and ended the call. I thought we had been disconnected for some reason because she has never ended a call like that. I tried to call her back but she has not answered so far." There was anguish in Meg's voice, and for a moment, Maria thought that Louise's behaviour was selfish or at least incomprehensible, considering that Meg needed support and comfort, especially from her best friend.

"Meg, let's go somewhere where we can talk without being disturbed." Maria led Meg to the smallest meeting room on the ground floor used for conversations with parents. Maria closed the door and sat on a chair, while Meg put down her bag and sat next to her teacher.

"Meg, Louise asked me last Sunday if she could talk to me after the lesson on Monday. She looked worried but I thought it was about you and your situation. Maybe she was worried about the whole situation since her dad is the manager of the company where the murder took place. On Monday she was not in class, but today? Why not come to school? And why end your call that way? There is something wrong. I want to try to call her, but before doing it, how is your dad?" she didn't want to say that she had talked to Jason, so she lied, "Father Mark has told me that he has not signed his confession yet. That is a good thing, isn't it?"

Meg sighed and Maria could see that, even if the girl was trying to be courageous and support her family, she was really tired and she would have needed a little relief from her constant concerns.

"Yes, my dad has not signed but tomorrow the lawyer will be back, and…" her eyes filled with tears, "what shall we do? The detective told my mum that he would call us before tomorrow afternoon and to trust him, but we haven't heard from him yet and we are getting worried."

"If the detective promised to call you, he will surely do so, don't worry. Maybe he is reaching the conclusion of his investigation and he is waiting to call you so that he can give you good news. Unfortunately, in the meantime, the secretary of your dad's company has been attacked and this must have complicated things. Now, let's try to call Louise, OK?"

Meg gave Maria Louise's mobile phone number and Maria dialled it after saving it in her contacts. After a few rings, a voice that was more a whisper answered, "Who's speaking?"

"Louise, it's Miss Busati, your Italian teacher. I am here with Meg and we are worried. Can I help you?"

The line was abruptly disconnected. Now Maria was really worried because something was definitely wrong with Louise.

She immediately dialled Jason's number, but after a few rings, it went to voicemail. She preferred not to leave a message.

"Meg, now go home and don't worry. I will try to call Detective Grant later and I am going to talk to Father Mark before going home. When is the lawyer's appointment with your dad tomorrow?"

"It is at four p.m. My mum and I will be there so that we can be present and support him."

"I am sure that before that time you will receive news from the detective, OK? Come on, just a little more patience and everything will be cleared, I am certain!" she tried to sound encouraging but she was really anxious.

Meg left and Maria knocked on the door of Father Mark's study. He did not answer and Mrs Dawson told Maria that he had gone to the hospital to visit Miss Lewis.

Maria went home and tried to concentrate on the correction of her students' homework but her mind and her heart were with those two young girls who were certainly going through a predicament that was maybe beyond their strength and endurance.

She tried once more to call Jason, but without success. Had she gone too far when she had shown him her sadness? She suspected that he didn't answer because he wanted to discourage her from contacting him because the first time he had immediately answered.

She waited anxiously for the return of Father Mark from the hospital so that she could call him. She was feeling that she had to do something for Meg and Louise.

***

Jason went back from Oshawa to his office at the police station. He immediately summoned Detective Hogan and gave him the list Mr Martin had handed him.

"Please, David, check the people on this list. They are the participants of the convention in Oshawa where Kilton was last Thursday. Ask everyone if they remember having talked to Kilton between seven-thirty and nine-fifteen p.m. and if they remember the time of the conversation."

"Is there anything new in the case, Jason?"

"There are two things I am sure about. Cooper is not the murderer and can't have attacked Miss Lewis, Bill Tucker is not responsible for the attack, because he was being shadowed. But..." he added after a pause, "I am discovering something about Kilton that I definitely don't like. It's still early to point a finger at him, but let's investigate that side of the matter, OK? I would also like to find out if there is any connection between Tucker and Kilton. Do you still have those withdrawal documents with Cooper's signature?"

"Yes, Jason."

"I would like the signature to be examined by a handwriting expert. I would like you to take a sample of Brown's and Kilton's handwriting and have the expert compare them."

"OK, Jason. This should not be difficult. We have some papers written by Brown that were in his desk drawer and on a few of them there is Kilton's signature. I will do what you have asked immediately. By the way, Tucker is still being shadowed, but so far, he has just been in his garage all day!"

"Thanks, David. By the way, how is your wife? I hope she is better."

Jason Grant was like this, he never forgot if one of his agents had a problem, that was what Detective Hogan liked about his boss. He was detached and solitary but he respected and cared for his agents and always called them by their first names. One evening, while Jason was coming out of his office he noticed Hogan still at his desk with his face in his hands and a troubled look. He had stopped, sat down next to him and asked if anything was wrong. Hogan had instinctively told him that his wife had been diagnosed with cancer and that she would be operated on soon. Jason had remained with him for a few minutes and tried to comfort and encourage him, and from that evening, he had frequently asked him how his wife was.

"Thanks, Jason. She has finished her therapy and the doctors say she will soon be able to go back to work!" he smiled, thinking of the past months of worry for his wife.

"I am happy to hear this," Jason said with a smile, "Now I want to go back to Kilton's company. I have some questions for the receptionist who seemed quite cooperative yesterday!"

Jason stood up and left. Detective Hogan looked at him going away, and before closing the door of Grant's office, he looked at the beautiful smiling girl in the frame on Jason's desk. He knew who she was and what had happened to her but he had never dared to say anything to Jason because he had noticed that the detective frequently looked at the picture with sweetness and sadness in his eyes.

***

Jason parked his unmarked car in the customer car park of Kilton Company. He knew that Brian Kilton usually left his office at about five p.m. When he saw the dark car with Kilton on board turning around the corner from the garage, he got out of his car and entered the building. Luckily, the receptionist was still there and immediately smiled at him.

"Detective, I am sorry but Mr Kilton has just left," she said kindly.

"Actually, I wanted to talk to you. Have you got a moment for me?"

The receptionist looked around to see if somebody needed her assistance but it was a quiet moment in the showroom, so she opened the door of the back office where she had talked to Jason the day before and she let him enter before closing the door. She was not nervous; maybe the absence of Kilton put all the employees more at ease.

Detective Grant took out his mobile phone and showed her a photo of Bill Tucker. "Have you ever seen this man?"

"Yes, sir, he came here more than once, but he never went up to the offices. He waited here in the showroom and he generally talked to Brown."

"Just to Brown?" the detective asked.

"No, of course, he often spoke to Kilton too." She noticed the surprised reaction of the detective and quickly added, "I thought he was a customer or a supplier but I often wondered why he didn't go upstairs to the office, even if I sometimes invited him to do so."

Jason put the phone back into his pocket and simply said with a smile, "Thanks, Miss Stevenson. You were very kind."

And he left.. One more piece of the puzzle, one he had been looking for!

While he was driving back to the office his phone rang. He had also missed a call from earlier while he was arriving at the Kilton Motor Company. It was Maria. 'No,' he told himself, 'it is better to stay away from her... maybe later... maybe later.' He let the phone ring without answering.

***

Maria called Father Mark later in the evening. He immediately answered and told her that Miss Lewis was slowly recovering and the doctors were optimistic. He listened with apprehension to Maria's account of the events of the afternoon. He said that he would call Louise first thing the next morning but Maria could feel that he was really worried. She didn't mention her useless attempts to call Jason and he didn't mention the detective.

After a few minutes, they ended the call, both feeling that the following day would be crucial for the destiny of the people involved in the case.

Chapter 16

Thursday, September 25th

Jason, as he had done for the past two days, called the hospital while he was preparing breakfast before going to the office.

The nurse was really cheerful when she told him that Miss Lewis was much better, she was still under sedation, but the doctors were planning to wake her in the afternoon. Jason thanked her and said that he would visit her that evening to see if she was able to talk.

Before ending the call, the nurse added that a relative of Miss Lewis had called the day before to ask how she was. Jason started when he heard this because Miss Lewis had no relatives, apart from her mother who could not call the hospital and didn't know she was there. He asked whether it was a male or female voice and the nurse said it had definitely been a woman's voice. Grant was perplexed and wondered who could have called pretending to be a relative.

He immediately called Agent Hogan and ordered a policeman to be stationed outside Miss Lewis's room as soon as possible. Hogan said he would send someone straightaway.

After breakfast, Jason drove to the police station where Hogan reassured him that a policeman was already at the hospital. Jason thanked him and walked into his office but Hogan added, "Jason, I wanted to inform you that we have called almost all the names on the list you gave us yesterday. Nobody remembers having talked to Kilton and someone even recalls having seen him leave after the meetings, even if they wouldn't swear to it."

"Thanks, David! My puzzle is almost complete! I just need some evidence or maybe just Miss Lewis's testimony, hoping she has seen something!"

Hogan added, "I have given the withdrawal documents and a sample of Brown's and Kilton's handwriting to our expert. I hope he will be able to give me the results tomorrow morning at the latest."

"Thanks, David!"

***

Grace was working at the diner that morning but she felt so agitated she was afraid of doing something wrong. The detective had not called her yet, and even if she knew it was against the diner policy for waitresses, she had kept her mobile phone in the pocket of her apron and she hadn't turned it off. That call was too important, it didn't matter if her boss reproached her.

It was almost noon when her phone finally vibrated in the pocket. Luckily, she had just served the last customer and she had a few minutes so she told her workmate she needed to go to the toilet and she left the dining room. When she could answer, it had stopped ringing but she saw Detective Grant's ID and she called him back. He answered very quickly.

"Detective, I am so glad to hear you. You remember our appointment with the lawyer, don't you?" 'She was so agitated, poor woman,' Jason thought.

"Mrs Cooper, good afternoon, I am sorry for not calling earlier but I have been rather busy. Mrs Cooper, your husband must absolutely refuse to sign any confession. I can't explain right now but I think I have found the real culprit. Please, tell him not to sign. He must tell the lawyer that he would rather face a trial than sign a confession for what he didn't do!" Jason's voice, which was usually calm, was really excited now and Mrs Cooper said immediately, "Don't worry, Mr Grant. Today I will be there with Meg and we are going to support him. But yesterday he told me that, whatever you would suggest, he was convinced not to sign because he felt it was not fair."

"Your husband is absolutely right, Mrs Cooper. Be patient for a few hours and I hope I will be able to exonerate your husband completely!"

Mrs Cooper was glad she was on the phone because she didn't want the detective to see her crying.

With a choked voice she was just able to say, "Thanks, Detective. Thanks," and she ended the call because the emotion was overwhelming her. Grant smiled and hoped he would really be able to solve this case soon, especially for Cooper and his family who had suffered so much in the past week.

***

The lawyer, Mr Williams, was expecting a call that morning, not a pleasant call at all, but he just received a text at about midday, which was far from conciliatory.

"Remember what I have paid you for, Williams. Cooper MUST confess, no matter what you say to convince him. Otherwise, I will ruin you, believe me!"

He had never liked that man, so arrogant, so full of himself, so convinced he could control everything and everyone, but it was true that being his lawyer, he knew a lot and he had endorsed a lot of dealings that were far from legal. So he had a lot to lose if he didn't do what that man ordered. On the other hand, he had little hope of convincing Cooper to sign, if he had not done it immediately when he was still scared and shocked by what had happened.

Williams sighed, he didn't reply to the text and prepared himself for a battle with his 'client' that was more for his own interest than for the interest of the suspect he was supposed to defend.

***

Father Mark went to the hospital as soon as he was free, in the early afternoon.

That morning, he had called Louise but her father had answered saying that Louise was not well with a fever and a cough and she would be at home for a few days. As always, Mr Kilton was far from gentle and he was particularly eager to end the call, but that was his usual way, especially with people like Father Mark, whom he considered inferior to his social status.

He carried his rosary and his breviary so that, in his prayers, he could accompany that poor lonely woman who was going to wake up after a few days of sedation and unconsciousness, and at the same time, he could pray fervently for Andy, Meg and Grace. He had gone to visit Andy in prison again the day before and he had seen him improved and determined not to sign any confession. He hoped that this was one of his last days in prison because he didn't belong there and his family needed him.

Before leaving for the hospital he called Meg to encourage her.

"Thanks, Father Mark, thanks for your support. Miss Busati talked to me at school this morning and she is always so kind and worried for us. I promised to call her as soon as we leave the prison!"

"OK," the priest simply said. "I will be at the hospital with Miss Lewis, but I will call you as soon as I am free. Say hello to your mum for me, and rest assured, my thoughts and my prayers are with you today!"

He ended the call, he wanted to call Maria too but it was getting late and he promised himself to call her later.

***

Andy Cooper received his wife and daughter with a smile and embraced Meg with tenderness. He blinked away his tears, which were partly for concern and partly for the great relief of having his family with him. They didn't talk much while they were waiting for the lawyer. Grace told him what Detective Grant had recommended on the phone but Andy had already decided what to do even if he was comforted by the words of the detective.

The lawyer arrived punctually at four p.m., he was visibly nervous, and during their whole conversation he kept looking at his phone that was on the table next to him. He looked so terrified that it seemed he was afraid the cell would explode all of a sudden.

He was not pleased to see Andy's wife and daughter with him but he knew it was useless to protest and he smiled politely. During the conversation, he looked steadily at Andy and avoided the gaze of Grace and Meg.

"Mr Cooper, I hope you have reconsidered your position and this confession," he took out the paper with the confession from a folder he had laid on the table.

"Mr Williams," Andy said with respect, "I know you are certainly advising me for what you think is the best and I appreciate your efforts, but I just can't sign something that is not true. I didn't kill Steve, I didn't take that money, and the more I think about it, the more I think that there is a murderer who would never be caught if I declared myself guilty! Even more so after the aggression toward the secretary, Miss Lewis. I am sorry but this is my final decision!" Meg was so proud of her dad, so happy to be there for him, so glad she had a wonderful family and so hopeful everything would be all right soon! She looked at her mum who was smiling for the first time in a week!

The lawyer looked scornfully at Andy and said, "I have already told you that any decision is up to you. I have already said that you were found next to the body of Brown with a paper-knife in your hand that was the murder weapon, that some envelopes with money were found in your drawer and that you signed the withdrawal documents for that money, you were the auditor, you had access to the bank accounts. This is evidence, Mr Cooper, strong evidence in a court of justice, believe me…" the lawyer knew that all his words were useless now, that if that man wanted him to force Cooper to sign a confession he should have planted more false proof. Now it was too late, he realized that clearly.

"I am sorry, Mr Williams, I won't take any more of your time uselessly, and if you don't want to defend me in court, Father Mark has offered to find me another lawyer."

"Certainly I won't defend you in a court, Mr Cooper. I certainly don't want to ruin my reputation, defending a person who doesn't stand any chance!" the lawyer said with a vehemence that, for a moment, took Andy, Grace and Meg aback, because they didn't believe that a man of the law could show his irritation so plainly.

For a moment, Mr Williams glared at Andy without speaking, then he said, "That is your final word, I imagine!" he turned for the first time to Grace, " I hoped you could talk some sense into him. You'll see what you have to face!" turning again towards Andy he added in a scornful tone, "I wish you good luck, Mr Cooper"

But while he was storming out of the room he was sure that the person who was running out of luck was that man he had to call now and not Andy Cooper!

***

Alison was gradually waking up and she found herself in a hospital bed. She had a strong headache and she felt confused, but gradually, she started to recall what had happened: the last thing she remembered was that dark figure, a man, who attacked her in her home. Now she looked around her and she saw a priest with a smiling face who was sitting on the chair next to the bed and a doctor and a nurse, watching her from the other side.

The doctor touched her gently on the shoulder and said, "Hello, Miss Lewis! How are you feeling?" He held her wrist to check her pulse for a few seconds.

She realized she had difficulty speaking and she had a heavy bandage around her head.

"I have a headache… But where am I? How long have I been here? Oh, my God, I have to visit my mum and pay..." her voice trailed off because she was starting to feel anxiety and apprehension.

The priest took her hand and caressed it soothingly, he put his breviary on the bedside table and said, looking at her with a comforting smile, "Hello, Alison! I am Father Mark the director of Miracle High School and the Catholic Parish Priest here in Trinity. Don't worry, now you have to recover and then you will think of everything else." Now she remembered Father Mark but it had been such a long time since she had been to the Sunday mass – The priest went on: "You have been here since last Monday night but the detective called the nursing home where your mum is staying and he told them what had happened..." he didn't know that Jason had paid the fee.

Alison looked around once more, trying to focus on what had happened, and at that moment, Jason Grant entered the room, he smiled at Father Mark and he approached the bed. Alison remembered the detective that had spoken to her the day after the murder. Now she was starting to put all her thoughts in order and focus...

The doctor looked at Jason and said, "Just a few minutes. Miss Lewis is still weak and needs to rest!" and he went out of the room, followed by the nurse.

Jason took a chair, sat down between the bed and Father Mark and said kindly, "Miss Lewis, I am glad you are recovering. You were badly hurt last Monday night. I don't want to disturb you now but I need to know if you remember anything..."

Alison said with an anguished voice, "My God, what day is it today? I had to pay for my mom's assistance. What can I do now?"

Jason was forced to admit, even if he didn't want to, "Miss Lewis, don't worry, I saw the bill at your home and I advanced the money." Father Mark smiled. This was Jason, this was the Jason he was so fond of, always ready to help, always sympathizing with the people who were suffering.

Jason went on, "I called the nursing home and your mum doesn't know anything about your attack. Now relax, and when you feel up to it, you will call and talk to your mum to reassure her, OK?" He saw that Alison was visibly comforted by what he was saying.

"Detective, you shouldn't have paid. I will give you the money back as soon as I can," she said as tears of gratitude were coming to her eyes.

Jason was deeply moved by this woman, whose first and only thought was her mum and he took her hand.

"Miss Lewis, can you tell me what you remember? Then we will leave you rest for a while... Miss Lewis tried to concentrate on her last day before her aggression and spoke slowly because she still had difficulties collecting her thoughts. Her account was interrupted by frequent pauses and it was painful to see the effort it cost her to talk.

"On Monday morning I remember talking to Mr Kilton... I told him that I had seen Brown put the two envelopes full of money into the drawer of Andy's desk... I think it was the day before the murder... He, Mr Kilton,

I mean,… he seemed indifferent and he told me that it meant nothing but that, if I wanted to go to the police, I could certainly do so… During lunch break he asked me to prepare some important documents… so I had to stay in the office and I couldn't go to the police station… I decided to go the following day… In the evening I arrived home… did the same things as usual. I was watching TV when my doorbell rang… instinctively I opened it a bit to see who it was…" her expression reflected the terror she had experienced. "A man seized my arm and jerked the door open… I tried to escape but he hit me…" here she stopped still trembling with fear at the remembrance of the aggression.

She resumed after a few moments, "I am sorry but I didn't see who it was, a man certainly, but I had not switched on the light in the foyer and it was dark."

Jason tried not to show his disillusionment at the impossibility of identifying the aggressor, but smiled at the sweet lady who was visibly still confused and said, "Now you have to rest, Miss Lewis, I will come to visit you again tomorrow."

Father Mark stood up and said gently, "I will come too if it gives you comfort, Alison."

She answered heartily, "Thanks, Detective Grant for your kindness. Thanks, Father. Yes, I have no relatives and I would like to see you again. Father, I would like you to visit my mum if you can. I don't go to church but she is very religious and I think hearing what has happened to me from a priest would be more comforting. I am afraid I won't be able to visit her for some time!"

Father Mark promised to go there the next morning and he left with Jason.

***

Maria was waiting anxiously for Meg's phone call. She wanted to know if everything was OK, if Andy had resisted the insistence of the lawyer. Time passed and Meg had not called yet. She and her mum had certainly gone back home by that time, it was getting late. Maria took her mobile phone and dialled Meg's number... no answer... then she dialled the Coopers' home phone number... no answer. What had happened? Her apprehension increased. She knew that Father Mark was at the hospital because Miss Lewis was better and he wanted to be beside her when she woke up. She decided to take a walk to calm down, then she would try again.

She tried once again to call Jason, but he did not answer!

***

When she came back after a short walk, which had not contributed to soothing her growing apprehension, Maria waited and waited. She tried again to call Meg and her mum but she got no answer. On an impulse, she decided to go to Meg's home and reassure herself that they were alright.

She took her car and drove to the Coopers'. While she was parking in front of the house her phone rang. It was Louise's number. She answered immediately, "Hi, Louise!"

The voice on the other end was anguished and extremely nervous and she had difficulty at first understanding what she was saying, because what she was hearing was a stream of incoherent words.

"Miss Busati, I am Katie, Louise's housekeeper, Mr and Mrs Kilton have gone mad. I don't know what to do. I have tried to call the school, Father Mark and Louise's uncle but nobody answers… Meg doesn't answer the phone… She is in danger. Call the detective, please."

"Miss Katie, please, I can't understand anything. Try to calm down and explain what is happening. I am in front of Meg's home. What's up?"

"Oh, my God! Mrs Kilton has gone to the hospital to kill the secretary, Mr Kilton has gone to do something, I don't know what, to Meg and her mum because he wants Meg's dad to sign a confession. Louise is here with me and I am afraid because she is trembling violently, she is in a state of panic, and she says she wants to talk to the police because she has seen everything. Miss Busati, she says she knows who killed Brown… what can I do?"

Maria said, "Does Mr Kilton have a dark car?"

Katie answered, "Yes, don't tell me he is there. Oh my God…"

Maria said, "Stay there with Louise, I will get in touch with the detective or the police. I will let you know…"

Maria frantically dialled Jason's number but he didn't answer. She dialled Father Mark's mobile phone number immediately, and luckily he answered. "Maria, are you OK? Have you heard from Meg?"

"Mark, I have just heard from Louise's housekeeper. She is at home with Louise. She said Louise knows who killed Brown. She told me that Mrs Kilton is going to the hospital to kill Miss Lewis and that Mr Kilton wants to force Meg's dad to sign the confession. He is here at the Coopers' because his car is parked here. I have tried to talk to Jason but he doesn't answer. Can you reach him, please?" her voice was upset and she hoped she had explained everything clearly enough. Father Mark looked for a moment at Jason disapprovingly because, while they were coming out of the hospital, he had heard Jason's phone ring and Jason had looked at the caller ID and had not answered. While Maria was talking he had put her on speaker and Jason had listened to what she had said. Now Jason said,

"I am here with Mark, Maria, I am sorry. Where are you now?"

"I am in front of the Coopers'. There is a dark car parked…" the phone call was abruptly interrupted.

Jason called the agent who was in front of Miss Lewis's room and he said that Kilton's wife had asked to see Miss Lewis and he had let her in. He ordered him to enter the room immediately. A few moments later, the agent told him that he had arrested Kilton's wife because she was standing next to the bed with a syringe in her hand.

In the meantime, Jason had called the police station to ask for reinforcements to be sent to the Coopers' home telling them to check the situation. He tried to call Maria back but she didn't answer.

Father Mark gave him Louise's phone number and Jason called her. Katie answered and he told her to stay at home because he would go to them immediately to see what Louise knew. Katie repeated that Louise was frightened and on the verge of hysteria.

Father Mark went back to his parish and Jason promised to call him as soon as he had news.

***

Maria was so intent on her conversation on the phone that she had not noticed a man approaching her car with a gun. While she was talking, she saw a gun pointed at her through the car window. She was so scared she didn't find the energy to cry for help and she just hung up. The man opened the car door and said sarcastically,

"Well, well, here is the famous Italian teacher my daughter loves so much! Come with me and give me that phone."

Maria had no other choice but to give him her mobile and get out of the car. The man took her by the arm and led her to the home. When they entered, she saw Meg and her mum sitting on the sofa with their hands and feet bound with a rope and a gag over their mouths. They looked petrified with terror. Maria was led by this man to sit on the other sofa next to them but the man didn't bind her. He had a sneer on his face. He turned off Maria's phone and threw it on the coffee table. He sat down on a chair he had taken from the kitchen and looked at them for a few moments.

"Now I didn't want visits, but maybe the teacher will serve my purposes as well." He looked at her with a dirty look as if he was judging her appearance from head to toe. "Not bad," he said in the end, "a great improvement from that old teacher Louise had."

He turned his attention back to Meg and her mum, "Now I will tell you once again what I want and I want it quickly. You have to call the prison, ask to talk to your husband and tell him to write and sign a confession. You must tell him that I will kill both of you and the teacher if he doesn't. Is everything clear?"

Meg and her mum nodded desperately.

Kilton stood up from the chair and approached Grace. When he was in front of her, he bent and said, "Now, if you promise to behave and not to shout, Mrs Cooper, I will take away the gag from your mouth, so that you can call, is it clear?"

Grace nodded and Kilton did as he had said. Then he handed her her phone, and said, "Now make that phone call!"

Grace said imploringly, "I don't have the number of the prison! I have never called the prison!" Kilton seemed to lose his patience and Grace was really scared but then he looked at his mobile for a minute and then said,

"Here it is, I found it on the internet." He let her see a phone number on his mobile phone and repeated, "Call NOW!"

Grace dialled the number she was given and put the phone on speaker. A professional voice answered. She asked to talk to her husband and she explained that it was urgent. The man on the other end said that she would have to wait for half an hour when the evening visiting time started. Grace thanked him and hung up, looking at Kilton who was visibly irritated.

***

When Jason arrived at the Kiltons' villa his phone rang, Hogan told him that he was in front of Meg's home with his agents who had already surrounded the house. Everything was still and there were no sounds coming from inside. Jason ordered him to wait until he had talked to Louise and to let him know if they heard anything. In reality, he had a plan in mind and he hoped it would work.

He got out of his car and since the gate was open, he walked up the drive to the house. The door was opened immediately by Katie, who had a frightened expression on her face.

"Detective Grant," Jason said showing his badge.

"Oh, Detective, please come in," Katie said and he entered through the large foyer into the enormous kitchen, where Louise was sitting on a chair, trembling uncontrollably.

Katie went to embrace Louise and said, "I don't know what to do, Detective. I can't calm her down and I am so worried. Mr and Mrs Kilton seemed mad… mad!!" she repeated.

An anguished voice said, "It's all my fault! It's all my fault! I should have gone to the police immediately…" Louise's voice was broken and she seemed on the verge of a nervous breakdown.

Jason knelt in front of her and took her hands, "Louise, it's not your fault, nothing is your fault, OK? We have already arrested your mum at the hospital! Look at me, Louise!"

Louise slowly raised her eyes and Jason said, "Now you are the only one who can save the life of your friend…" but Louise was shaking her head and still trembling, even if the warmth of the detective's hands that were holding hers was beginning to calm her down.

"What do you know?" Louise looked at him and took out of her sweatshirt pocket a mobile phone. She gave it to the detective.

"I found this in my dad's car, under the passenger seat, a few days after the murder…" she had to pause because what she was going to say next would change her life completely. She sighed and added, "The night of the murder I was coming home from the gym, that is behind my father's company, and I saw him come out of his company garage, wait in his car at the corner until Meg's dad's car arrived, wait for a few minutes and then make a phone call. Then he drove away. He didn't see me but I stopped to watch him because he should have been in Oshawa. The following days I tried to talk to him because I thought maybe there was an explanation, but he got angry, he kept me at home from school and he even beat me..." here Louise started to sob and showed Jason a bruise on her cheek.

Jason said, "Louise, I know it is hard for you, but I would like you to come with me to Meg's home. Your father is there and I suspect he is threatening Meg and her mum. I fear he has taken even your Italian teacher."

"But what can I do? My dad doesn't love me, now I know for certain, and he doesn't want to go to prison, he would do anything to avoid arrest!"

"Would you come with me, please, Louise? I would like you to try to speak to your dad. Would you do that for your friend? For your teacher?"

"Promise me you won't allow my dad to beat me or even to come near me!" she looked imploringly at Jason. He was really moved by this poor teenage girl who didn't want to meet her father and was scared of her father. 'A father is meant to protect a daughter, not to frighten her so much,' he thought.

"I promise, he won't hurt you. I won't let him do it. You have my word, Louise!"

Louise stood up from the chair and the detective put a protective arm around her shoulders, leading her to his car.

***

That half hour seemed an eternity to Kilton. He knew he was doing something desperate, he was not thinking clearly but one thing was perfectly clear in his mind; he didn't want to go to prison, he didn't want to lose all the money and the privileges he had accumulated, in part, honestly, but mostly, dishonestly. When had everything started to go wrong? That Brown, he was the weak link, he should have thrown him out of the company long before, but he was useful, he owed him so much money that he had to do what he was ordered. And that model of honesty, that Cooper... Why do such honest and irreproachable people exist? Why couldn't he be bought with money? But now it was too late, he had to stay out of prison.

His phone rang just a few minutes before the end of that half-hour. He looked at the ID; his daughter, Louise.

Instinctively he answered, at least he wanted to be sure she had not talked to anyone.

"Louise, what's the matter now?" he had never really gotten attached to that daughter, always asking for his attention, always so hardworking at school, almost too perfect.

On the other end of the line, a seemingly calm voice answered, "Dad, I want to talk to you. And now you have to listen to me, for the first time in my life!" there was something different in his daughter's voice, she seemed to have immediately become an adult, there was something compelling, an almost authoritarian tone in her voice that he had never heard. But then he had seldom listened to her. If he had heard the usual childish voice pleading with him to listen to her, he would have hung up, but this time it was different and he didn't, he couldn't for some reason.

His daughter continued, "I know you have never loved me, I know you have maybe not wanted me from the first, I have always irritated, angered and disappointed you. And the only thing I really wanted was the love of a family. Mum is in prison now and you are pointing a gun at my best friend. But even if you do something terrible once again, I want you to know that I am here with the police, I have told them everything I know and I have given them the mobile phone I found in your car." He had searched for that mobile phone for days. Kilton now was really starting to lose his self-confidence.

"I have tried to talk to you many times in the last few days, I had hoped against hope that you would explain and would come clean from this situation, but now I just want you to know that I am ashamed of you, I never want to talk to you again, I am sorry you are my father. So you see, you have no way out. So why kill other people, innocent people like Brown and Mrs Lewis?" Louise wondered if he was still listening. It was the longest speech she had ever made to her dad without interruptions. She was also surprised by her composure. What she was saying was what she really meant, her longing for the love of her parents was turning into hate.

Kilton couldn't believe that his daughter was disobeying his orders. He had always thought that his daughter would do what he ordered. But what was she talking about? Love? What could he do? For a moment, he stared in front of him towards the window and turned his back to his three hostages. Maria saw that he was not looking at them and saw the silhouette of a man, a policeman certainly, in the glass front door. She took the courage to move quickly to the door to open it. When he recovered from his trance, Kilton saw Maria opening the door, and on a last desperate impulse, he shot in her direction. Maria felt herself being pushed aside by strong arms and the bullet missed her. Those strong arms belonged to Jason who had approached the house while Louise was talking on the phone. Grant ordered Kilton to raise his arms immediately. Now it was really over. He threw his gun to the floor and an agent, who had entered behind Jason, picked it up and put handcuffs on Kilton, leading him away. Another agent, a woman, came in and went to the sofa to unbind Meg and her mum and to take care of them.

Jason put his gun back in the holster attached to his belt and turned to look at Maria. She was in a corner terrified. He had saved her life. He put an arm around her shoulders and led her to the sofa next to the one where Meg and her mum were lost in an embrace of love and relief. She sat down and he bent in front of her. He told the female officer to go get a glass of water for her and he took her hands in his.

"Maria," he said, not caring if Meg and her mum heard that he called her by her first name, " I have behaved like a fool and I am really sorry. Are you OK?"

Maria knew what he was talking about, but she said simply, "You don't have to apologize, you have just saved my life, Jason, thanks!" What was that strange impulse she was feeling and she was resisting embracing him? "I am alright… just a bit shaken, I think!"

She embraced Meg and Grace and Jason left them for some minutes. The policemen wanted to call a doctor but the three women said they were OK. Then, when Jason was sure they had all recovered from the shock, he offered to drive Maria home but she said she had her car and she was feeling better now. Jason didn't insist because he was afraid his emotions would have the upper hand and would make him do or say something he would later regret. Nevertheless, he ordered an officer to drive Maria home in her car.

***

In the car, sitting on the passenger seat next to Jason, Louise felt safe as she had never felt in her life so far. When they arrived at Meg's home, Jason told her to take her mobile phone and to call her dad; she had to try to convince him to give up, to surrender.

After she had talked to her father, she felt a strange sense of relief. She had finally been able to say what had weighed on her heart for a long time.

Jason had been next to her and then he had approached the front door of the Coopers' home, and after a few minutes and one gunshot, she had seen her father come out handcuffed. She had not felt any sympathy for him, she had just watched him as he got into a police car.

Someone behind her, someone she knew very well, called her name, "Louise!" She turned and saw her Uncle Joseph and his wife, Isabel, next to Father Mark who was smiling at her. She ran into her uncle's arms and she knew, from that moment, her life would change completely. She didn't look back, she just wanted to go with her uncle and aunt who had always loved her as their daughter.

She looked gratefully at Father Mark. When he had arrived at the Parish he could not remain calm, he couldn't even pray. He had looked for the number of Joseph Kilton and he had called him. Joseph had just arrived from Vancouver and the priest had waited for him in front of the church and had guided him to the Coopers'.

For some minutes Louise just enjoyed the embrace and the affection of her aunt and uncle, then she said with a voice choked with emotion, "Uncle Joseph, I am so happy you are here! I am sorry but I had to tell the police what I saw. I know he is your brother…" her voice trailed off. Her uncle embraced her and said, "You have done the right thing, Louise! Now come home with us!" Jason had reached them and said, shaking Uncle Joseph's hand,

"You can be very proud of your niece, Mr Kilton! She contributed to saving the lives of her friend, Meg, her mum and her Italian teacher."

Louise asked for permission to say hello to her friend and Jason allowed her to go into the home with her uncle. Maria was still there too.

While Louise was with Maria, Meg and her mum, Father Mark took the chance to tell Jason, "We'll have to talk one of these days, Jason. Why didn't you answer when Maria called? Was it the first time? Jason, you could have put her life in great danger by not answering, you know that, don't you?"

Jason cast his eyes down and said in a low voice, "You are right, Mark. The fact is that..." he stopped and added quickly, "I promise I'll come to you as soon as I have concluded this investigation. Then you can tell me off as much as you like. I deserve it, I know," he added with a smile.

Chapter 17

Friday, September 26th

Maria woke up the following morning after a good night's sleep. As soon as she had got home the previous evening, she had made herself a cup of coffee and she had put on her pyjamas. While she was going to bed, she received a phone call from Meg, who wanted to know if everything was OK and said that she and her mum would be at the police station the following morning to sign their deposition. Maria had said she would be there for the same reason too. She had chatted with Meg and her mum for a few minutes and then, as soon as she had gone to bed, she had fallen asleep.

While she was preparing breakfast, she received a message from Jason, 'I hope you slept well and you feel fine this morning. See you later at the police station.' She smiled, even if the thought of Jason aroused in her mixed feelings; on one side, she told herself that they had seldom spoken to each other and that she couldn't believe he had any interest in her, on the other side, she kept wondering why he had avoided her. This hurt her because she didn't think she had been insistent or inopportune. She hoped to be able to talk to him, to clarify everything, because she couldn't deny she was starting to feel something for that sensitive, sad man and she needed to know what his feelings were.

After breakfast, she took a shower and got dressed. She was ready to go to the police station.

***

The police station was very busy that morning. Meg and her mum were there, Louise with her uncle and aunt arrived, and when they were all gathered, waiting for the officer who should take their depositions, Maria entered the room. Louise immediately introduced her to her uncle. Maria noticed with pleasure that Louise was completely different; she was more lively and more confident, evidently, the lack of affection in her family had weighed on her for a long time and her uncle and aunt were able to give her the warmth and the love she needed. It was evident she loved her aunt and uncle and they were very fond of their niece.

Joseph Kilton shook hands with Maria and said warmly, "Louise has spoken so much about you! I am sorry for what my brother has done and for what he could have done if the detective had not intervened in time," he added with a sad expression, "I have always told him that he was too greedy, and his wife certainly didn't help him."

Maria said simply, "Don't worry, Mr Kilton. I see Louise is so happy with you. That is the most important thing!" She smiled at Louise, who was looking at her with admiration.

Meg embraced her teacher and said, "You were very courageous yesterday. We are sorry you were involved but we could not call you to warn you!"

"Don't worry, Meg! But how is your dad? When is he coming out of prison?"

Grace said, "After our deposition, we are going to pick him up. We are so happy! Detective Grant told us yesterday that the judge would send the documents for his release this morning! Oh, I still can't help thinking what would have happened to you, Miss Busati, if the detective had not arrived in time!"

Maria felt a little embarrassed because she was aware that the previous evening they had called each other by their first names. She didn't know what Meg and her mum would think. But she didn't care, she knew that the Coopers were reserved people.

"I know," Maria said, "he saved my life. I think I will have to cook something special for him," she added with a smile, in order to release the tension, mostly her tension and uneasiness at the thought of the detective. The others laughed heartily.

Uncle Joseph said, " Yes, I think delicious Italian dishes are a good way to express gratitude!" Now they were all smiling and relaxed. While they were talking, they heard the unmistakable voice of Jason coming from the other room. He opened the door but… who was with him?

Meg couldn't believe her eyes, in front of her was her dad, her hero. Andy was smiling, even if his face was still drawn and tired. She ran into his arms and Grace followed her. Jason, before coming to the police station, had gone to the court to take the documents for the release and then to the prison to pick up Andy.

Jason was smiling, knowing that he had made a great gift to this wonderful family, after so much suffering. He invited Louise, her uncle and aunt and Maria to go into another room so that Andy and his family could enjoy a few moments of privacy.

An officer came and asked Louise to go with her relatives into an office to read and sign the deposition. Louise embraced Maria and said,

"See you this afternoon at school, Miss Busati."

"Of course," Maria said and she took her leave of Mr and Mrs Kilton.

Jason smiled at Maria and invited her into his office to read and sign the deposition. An officer took Maria's documents and made a copy and Jason and Maria sat down.

Jason remained professional while they were reading and signing the statement. He said, "I hope that Kilton will be more reasonable today after a night in prison! Yesterday he kept on repeating we had no proof and he hadn't done anything!"

Maria replied, "But in the time he was waiting for Grace to call the prison, he deliberately said that he didn't want to be arrested and he admitted to his crime. And then he can't deny trying to kill me! Is his confession necessary?"

Jason sighed and said, "We have Louise's testimony that he came out of the company a few minutes before the arrival of Cooper and on his prepaid phone we found the call to the police. We arrested his wife yesterday for the attempted murder of Miss Lewis. We have the testimony of the Kiltons' housekeeper that yesterday he and his wife discussed what they could do to avoid prison. However, I would like him to confess because he could keep on denying the aggression to Miss Lewis, who didn't see her attacker." He paused for a few moments and then he instinctively looked at the young girl in the picture on his desk. He went on as if speaking more to himself than to Maria, " But if you had heard what Louise told her dad on the phone yesterday. Any father would have felt ashamed of himself for much less!"

"Louise hasn't had a father all these years! This is very sad, I think!" Maria replied and thought of her stepfather, who for her had been a real affectionate loving dad. When Jason had handed the signed document to an officer who made a copy for her, he looked at Maria and said, "Maria, first of all," Maria noticed that he was embarrassed and shy and she felt a wave of tenderness for that man who risked his life every day and had difficulty speaking to a woman he hardly knew. "First of all, I have to apologize for my behaviour in the last few days. I have not answered your calls and this is inexcusable and impolite, to say the least."

Maria's gaze fell on that smiling young girl in the frame and she said, "You were working and I shouldn't have called you. You have no reason to apologize, we have just met and we have only talked in relation to Meg's situation. You don't know anything about me and I don't know anything about you." She realized she was sounding more detached than she really wanted to be because, in reality, she was eager to know who that girl in the photo was. A girlfriend? A daughter? 'No, Maria,' she told herself, 'you can't expect a man like him to be here waiting for you. He certainly has relations.' What was funny was that Jason was thinking the same thing, 'No, Jason, a charming woman like her is not waiting for you. She can find a more fascinating, more handsome, more pleasant man than you! Or maybe she has someone in Italy ready to reach her in Canada.'

Jason had noticed her gaze and he looked at the photo with his usual tender expression. Then he turned to Maria and said,

"Maria, what you have just said is true, but if it is OK with you, I would like to talk to you and get to know you better. I owe you at least an explanation for my behaviour, even if maybe it meant nothing to you." Maria replied, without thinking,

"No, your behaviour hurt me, but I don't want you to feel obliged to explain if it is difficult for you." Her voice trailed off because she had just admitted indirectly that she was interested in him.

Jason smiled and went on, "Now I have to go to the interrogation room to speak to Kilton. But if you allow me when this is all finished, I would like to come to you to talk about a thing…" he stopped and looked at Maria with a troubled expression as if he was debating within himself what to do.

"Jason, you don't owe me any explanation! I am sorry for saying it hurt me when you didn't answer. You saved my life yesterday and I am grateful but I only called you in the last few days because I was worried for Louise and Meg and… you mustn't feel obliged or forced to…"Her voice trailed off because, the more she talked, the more she realized she was saying the contrary of what she was feeling and she was longing to get to know this man better.

"But I want to talk to you!" Jason said with force, "I have to find the courage to tell you something! Let me get rid of this investigation and then…" His face reflected the struggle he was experiencing after six years of isolation, of silent suffering.

Maria stood up and left hastily because she was afraid she would embrace this man if she stayed. Jason aroused in her feelings of tenderness, respect and… love! But what was so difficult for him to tell her?

Jason remained in his office for a few minutes after Maria had left. Would he be able to open his heart to her, to tell her what had made him suffer for six years, the meaning of that picture on his desk?

Hogan knocked on his office door and brought him back to his job. "Hi, David! Have you talked to Tucker?"

"Yes, Jason. He has admitted that he had dealings with Kilton. He sold him stolen and low-quality car spare parts and he mounted these parts in the cars Kilton would sell. Kilton paid Brown's debts and Brown, in exchange, had to hide the transactions so that the name of Tucker would never be mentioned. Last summer, Brown evidently made a mistake. He got nervous and as a part of their deal, Kilton asked him to plant evidence against Cooper. Tucker doesn't know what happened next, but the most educated guess is that Brown tried to back out and Kilton couldn't let that happen."

"This adds up, but what about Miss Lewis? What does Tucker know?"

"Kilton called Tucker because he wanted him to kill Miss Lewis, but Bill knew he was being shadowed and said he wouldn't do it. He says he doesn't know anything else because he has not heard from Kilton since last Monday."

Jason asked, "And what about Mrs Kilton? What does she have to say?"

Hogan said, smiling, "I think she is overwhelmed by her situation now, so different from all the luxury she has always lived in. She doesn't speak, she has only said that she couldn't allow that woman, she means Miss Lewis, to ruin her life. She has not asked for her daughter, she has not asked how Louise is, nothing, Jason. Is that a mother?" Jason shook his head sadly.

"OK, thanks, David. Has Kilton been brought to the interrogation room?"

"Yes, he is there with his lawyer when you want. I think he is a little less arrogant than yesterday."

"I hope he has reflected on his daughter's words." He paused and added, "David, when a teenage girl asks you not to let her father come near her and shows you the bruises on her face and says her dad has beaten her… I feel a sense of repulsion for such a man. I will have to keep calm because this is the kind of man that makes me nervous."

"You are absolutely right, Jason, and he could have killed that Italian teacher without even thinking about it! Thank God you arrived in time." Hogan pretended not to see the expression on the face of his boss at his mentioning Maria. Was it tenderness? Was it respect? Love, maybe? No, he had never believed the tough Jason Grant he knew would ever show love.

While Jason was putting his gun into the locker before going to the interrogation room, Hogan called him and said, "Jason, there is someone who wants to say goodbye to you before leaving!"

He didn't have time to turn because two happy teenage girls ran to him and embraced him. Hogan watched his tough boss, seldom smiling, visibly embarrassed but also pleased at this demonstration of love and gratitude. Jason smiled at the two girls and behind them, he saw Mr and Mrs Kilton and Mr and Mrs Cooper. The reward for his investigation was seeing these six people really happy and relieved.

Meg spoke first, "Detective Grant, I wanted to thank you. I will never forget the way you comforted me that evening when I was so desperate and worried. Thanks for your words and for believing in my dad's innocence… and…" she added with a smile, "Thanks for saving the life of our Italian teacher!" Jason felt himself blushing at the name of Maria but he tried not to show his embarrassment.

Louise added, "Thanks for letting me talk to my father. I realized that it was my chance to tell him what I thought. Thanks for comforting and calming me down. Thanks, Detective Grant, for protecting me…" her voice was full of emotion. In the end, she was the one who had suffered the most since she was born. Jason looked into Louise's eyes and said,

"You were very courageous, Louise, and you saved the life of your friend and her family. Now you must try to forget and live happily with your uncle and aunt, OK?" The girl looked at him and nodded solemnly.

Andy Cooper approached him and said, "When they told me that terrible night that you would come to interrogate me, I was scared. I had heard that you were tough and severe but…" he paused before adding, "I discovered a sensitive and human person and I will never forget the support you gave to my family. Thanks, Detective!"

Isabel and Joseph Kilton shook hands with Jason and Isabel said, "Thanks, Detective. We hope my brother-in-law will have time to reflect in prison. He has done so much wrong especially to Louise." She looked with affection at her niece.

Jason was not used to talking much and he was always embarrassed when someone praised or thanked him because he truly believed that he was just doing his job. Now, he simply said,

"Seeing you happy and relaxed after so much stress, suffering and worry is the best reward for me. Mrs Kilton, I am going to talk to your brother-in-law now, I hope he will really and deeply understand the gravity of his actions, but most of all, the suffering he has caused to Louise, his wickedness to her." With these words, he took leave of the two families.

Hogan watched him leave and told Andy Cooper, "Jason is very tough with criminals and people who don't respect human life but I can assure you he is one of the most sensitive and considerate people I know." He smiled and added, "You must never believe what people say."

***

On Kilton's face, you could easily see the effect of a night in prison. He was no more the haughty, arrogant and self-confident man Grant had seen in his office.

Jason prayed he would be able to stay calm because Kilton irritated him enormously.

The lawyer was sitting beside Kilton with a solemn face. He was not the counsellor Kilton had sent to Cooper, he was a man in his late sixties, bald with thick glasses and a grey moustache.

Detective Grant entered the same room where he had spoken to Cooper a week before and he sat down in front of the two men who were waiting for him.

He asked simply, "What can you tell me, Kilton? We have already spoken to Tucker who told us about your dealings, we had a handwriting expert analyse the signature of Cooper on those withdrawal statements and he confirmed that the signature was forged. We had him compare that signature to a sample of your and Brown's handwriting and he has confirmed that it was you who forged it. The testimony of the expert is in the documents I have given to your lawyer. Now, I want to hear what you have to say."

Kilton looked at his lawyer and then he turned to Grant: "What I have to say, Detective? What YOU have to say, YOU have forced my daughter to call me, to disobey me. My daughter has always done what I have ordered, you have put her against me. Did you write down for her that little speech she made on the phone?" he asked sarcastically.

Grant had promised himself to stay calm but this was too much. He slammed his fist on the table and leaned towards Kilton. He refrained from touching him, only because the lawyer was present, but his voice added emphasis to what he said next, "Kilton, if we want to talk about your dealings with Brown and Tucker, OK! But leave your daughter out of it. Your daughter was trembling uncontrollably when I arrived at your home yesterday night, she had bruises on her face and your housekeeper confirmed you had beaten her and it was not the first time. She implored me in front of the housekeeper and then again in front of my agents not to let you go near her." The lawyer was changing his expression completely. He turned to his client and said,

"Mr Kilton, you hadn't told me anything about this. You had better not say anything more!" He was evidently disappointed. Grant went on because now he wanted to make this man really ashamed of himself if he was even able to feel shame.

"She gave me your prepaid phone willingly because I didn't know anything about it. I gave her her phone and she accepted it to call you. What she said on the phone was what maybe she had wanted to tell you for all these years. She is not a puppet, Kilton, she is a sweet teenage girl, who has never had a real father and mother, a caring father and mother. I was shocked by what she was telling you. At least show some decency at leaving her out of it."

Kilton was taken aback and he reproached himself for having mentioned Louise. Why had he and his wife had their daughter? If it hadn't been for her… Now it was all over, he knew. His wife was in prison and he would go to jail. Maybe if he confessed…

"OK, Detective. It was all Brown's fault. He was a weak man and I knew from the beginning that he was not to be trusted. And then that Cooper, the most honest person in the world. What did I have to do? I have a company to manage and everybody knows that when you are a manager like me, you have to accept compromises if you want to make your firm prosper. I ordered Brown to plant evidence against Cooper, but I knew that he would never do it, so I came back from Oshawa and heard him call his colleague... What else could I do?" Jason looked at him disparagingly, Kilton was constantly trying to find excuses and justifications, he would never deal with his errors.

"And Miss Lewis?" Grant pressed on.

"She had seen Brown put the money into Cooper's drawer. She wanted to go to the police. Maybe she had heard something because she was my secretary. I couldn't afford to let her talk."

Jason took a deep sigh, at least now Kilton had confessed to both the murder and the aggression. "Why didn't Cooper accept to sign a confession? I would have given his wife and daughter money and he would have spent a few years in prison. Why couldn't the people do what I ordered!"

Grant could have remained silent but he had to say, "Because people don't love you, Kilton, they are just afraid of you. Your employees, your daughter, your housekeeper. And your wife only loves your money and your social position. Your daughter feels protected by a policeman she has never met before and she doesn't feel safe in her own family. You are the most miserable man in the world, Kilton, let me tell you this." The lawyer said nothing. He just gathered his papers and his bag and stood up, preparing to leave.

***

Father Mark was waiting for Jason that evening after Vespers in Church. The detective had announced he would be there after a busy day completing his report on the case he had just closed. When he arrived, he went directly to Mark's study. He knocked on the door and the priest let him in. The priest invited him to sit down and he went to sit in the armchair next to Jason.

"Hi, Mark. How are you?" This was always his first question, no matter why he was talking to the priest or how much time he had to talk.

Father Mark looked at this tall detective, now forty-three-years-old, whom he had known as a schoolboy in Toronto. He admired him for his honesty, his rectitude, his professionalism in his job, and also for the way he was enduring this suffering and sense of guilt that had been tormenting him for six years. He had prayed so much for Jason's serenity, for relief from his remorse. He loved him as a son, he had accompanied him through a life of satisfaction and successes in his job but of great losses.

Jason was looking at him with the admiration he had always felt for his priest friend. Mark had always been there for him, in his moments of joy and in times of desperation, always ready to help him, and now he needed his advice so much!

"I am fine, Jason, next month I will have my usual annual check-up, but I feel all right now!" Jason smiled because the sudden illness of the priest had been a cause of great apprehension. "Tell me, the case is closed, has Kilton confessed?"

Jason sighed and said, "Mark, one of the saddest moments in my career was yesterday night when I talked to Louise. She was really scared of her dad, he had even beaten her and... what she told her dad on the phone! She was talking like an adult, putting in front of her father all his failures as a parent, telling him plainly that he had never loved her and she knew. Poor girl! And this morning, she came with Meg to embrace me and thank me! I was really moved by these two teenagers who have always supported each other! Now Meg will go back to her serene family life, but Louise will have to forget a past life that has been really painful for her..." he paused for a moment and resumed, "Yes, Kilton has confessed, but always trying to justify himself as if what he has done was inevitable and necessary! I wonder if he will ever realize what he has done, not only to Brown but with his life and his family." Father Mark shook his head sadly and said,

"His way to change and redemption will be a long one!"

He turned to look at Jason and said, "You know, Jason, what I am going to tell you! Why didn't you answer Maria's phone calls? If you had answered immediately, maybe you could have spared her that danger, you know that, don't you?"

Jason cast his eyes down and didn't answer. Father Mark leaned forward in his armchair, put a hand on Jason's arm and said, "Jason, six years ago you made up your mind; you decided that isolation was a way to punish yourself for a guilt that is not yours." Jason was looking at him with a troubled expression and he was shaking his head in denial. "Yes, Jason, in your heart you know it was not your fault. Anyway, you chose isolation to protect the people you care for and I told you at that time that you would have to change your mind sooner or later, didn't I?"

Jason lifted his eyes and looked at the priest, after a few moments he nodded but he still didn't speak.

Father Mark resumed, "Not answering the phone is not a solution. Jason, now you have to think, you have to reflect… Do you care for Maria? Are you falling in love with her?"

An anguished voice interrupted him and said, "Mark, I can't, you know!"

"No, Jason, you are not condemned to remain alone. And you are a reliable trustworthy man, you are absolutely capable of loving and caring. Answer my question, Do you care for Maria?"

Jason sighed, he paused for a few moments and spoke slowly, as if every word cost him an effort, "Mark, last Monday when I went to her to talk about the Coopers and I saw her so sad I… yes, Mark, I care for her: I have never met such a sensitive, honest, caring, sweet woman and unwillingly, I have started to imagine myself with her." Jason stopped and buried his head in his hands. "No, Mark, I can't, I wouldn't stand another person suffering because of my job. I couldn't stand to lose her."

"Jason, but if you love her, you will not be able to stay away from her. During these six years, you have remained alone because you haven't found a person you really cared for but I knew that, sooner or later, you would have to come to terms with your grief. Do you think you could avoid meeting her?" he smiled and added, "Because I am telling you now that I don't intend to send her back to Italy next year. She is a wonderful teacher and I will offer her a permanent contract. Do you think you could stand seeing her maybe going out with a colleague? She is an attractive woman and one or two of the other teachers have already started asking her out…" he paused and then said, "You know that I have never interfered with your decisions, but if you think that Maria, and I believe you are right, is a sensitive, sweet girl you have to reflect; if your heart tells you that you love her, as I think you do, talk to her, open your heart to her, remember that no relationship should be based on secrets. And doing what you have done in the last few days can only hurt her and keep her at a distance. Is this what you want? Maria is wise enough to decide what she wants to do and what is better for her and for you. Once you have told her what weighs on your heart, from her reaction you will see if she is the one who is meant to be! And give a little credit to the Divine Providence too! That never fails, I can assure you!" he added with a smile.

"Mark, I will do what you suggest. I will reflect and make up my mind because, you know, Maria would be the first person I tell what happened. Please, Mark, pray for me because tomorrow I will either talk to Maria or decide to go on alone. But this will be an important decision for me and you know more than anyone else! But…" he reflected before adding, "you said you will offer her a permanent job here, but what if she decides to go back to Italy? Maybe her family…"

"Jason, you know I never talk about other people. If you open your heart to her, she will certainly do the same with you, but let me just tell you that she is very lonely and that she doesn't have strong bonds with Italy now. Jason, I will pray for you but I am sure that you will find the right way. Love always guides us on the right path."

Father Mark watched Jason leave and smiled because he was sure that there was a person now who was finding her way to the heart of this tough policeman and he would no longer be alone.

Chapter 18

Saturday September 27th

The Kiltons and the Coopers had planned a visit to Miss Lewis in the early afternoon of Saturday. She was still in hospital but she was recovering quickly and the doctors planned to release her the next Tuesday after a check-up.

When they arrived, they found Father Mark who was talking to Alison. When he saw the two families enter, he stood up from the chair where he was sitting. Louise and Meg embraced the priest they had known for a few years, who they loved. Alison was visibly happy to see Andy. He was the one who went to the bed to embrace her,

"Alison, I am so happy to see you are recovering! I was so sad when they told me about the attack. How are you?" Alison smiled and said,

"Now that I see you out of prison I am much, much better, thanks. I was so worried for you, Andy!" Louise and Meg came near the bed and they shook hands politely with the lady, followed by Isabel and Grace.

Andy asked, "How is your mum? Have you been able to call her?"

Father Mark said, "I went to visit her yesterday and she was worried because she had not seen her daughter. We have just called her and now she is relieved because she has heard Alison's voice and she is comforted by the thought that Alison is better and will soon be able to visit her."

"Father Mark, you must promise me to tell Detective Grant that I will pay him back as soon as I am out of hospital!" Alison said with emotion in her voice. She turned to the other visitors and said, "The detective saw the bill from the nursing home on my table the day after the aggression and he paid it for me! Who says that he is cold and detached?"

Father Mark smiled and replied, "I know he has this reputation here in Trinity because people know that he has arrested dangerous criminals in Toronto and all over Canada and because, when they meet him in town, he is always serious and of few words. He is certainly detached and tough with criminals but never with victims and," he added, "knowing him as I do, he wouldn't like you to tell everyone what he has done, Miss Lewis!"

She laughed and said, "Oh, but I will tell everybody, I don't care if he doesn't like it! But Father, he has such a sad look in his eyes, even when he smiles. I hope he doesn't have a sick relative or something like that!"

Father Mark sighed at the thought of the tragedy that had struck twice the life of his friend, he thought that it was high time someone made that sad look disappear.

He replied to Miss Lewis, "Every person has his or her cross to carry, big or small, heavy or light, Miss Lewis, and Detective Grant has been carrying his for a few years now." He left it at that. "Now I have to go back to my Parish, Alison. Remember, you promised to come to church one of the next Sundays," he added with a smile.

Alison replied, "I will remember my promise, Father, thanks for your support and for visiting my mum."

Father Mark said goodbye to Alison and her visitors and left.

Joseph Kilton approached the bed now and said, "Miss Lewis, I am really sorry for what my brother has done to you. I have already told Andy and I want to tell you that I intend to take over Kilton Motor Company. My father founded it many years ago and I decided to leave because I didn't get on with Brian. But now I want to manage it as my dad would have liked, without secret dealings and threats. I hope you will be my secretary, Miss Lewis." Alison couldn't believe it. In the past few days, she had been worried about her job and she had endured Brian Kilton's rude behaviour for many years because she needed her salary, but now… With watery eyes and a voice choked by emotion, she was just able to say,

"Thanks, Mr Kilton. Thanks so much."

The Kiltons and the Coopers remained for some time to keep the lady company, chatting about what had happened, but mostly, about plans for the future and the celebration of Andy and Grace's anniversary in two weeks.

***

Maria was really sad; she had hoped Jason would come to her or at least call her but it was Saturday afternoon and she had not heard from him yet. It was the first time she had felt this way. In her life, she had had a few boyfriends, but evidently, she had never found the real love of her life. What was happening now with a man she hardly knew? What did she see in Jason that she had not seen in any other man? He had been very kind, it is true, he had even saved her life thanks to his readiness but he had also refused to answer her calls. She was confused and restless, and before the evening mass, she decided to go for a walk at the lake. Walking had always succeeded in soothing her. She put on jeans and a light sweater, she took her bag and she left her home. She didn't know why but she had refused Julian's invitation to go to the cinema with him that evening, she just didn't feel like being with other people, not that evening.

She started to walk on the path that bordered the lake. The days were getting shorter and it was not so warm, but it was a pleasant late afternoon and the autumn leaves became golden in the sun. She was walking briskly and looking distractedly at the lake when she heard her name, but… that voice, "Maria!" she turned and instinctively she clutched the wedding ring hanging from her neck as if to ask for her dad's help because she knew this would be one of the most important moments in her life.

Jason stood there, smiling shyly at her, with his blazer in his hands, wearing a shirt with rolled-up sleeves and jeans, no gun, no badge. He seemed even taller, more handsome and his dark blue eyes reflected the light of the afternoon sun. Maria's heart started to beat faster, she stopped and he caught up with her.

"I have just been to your home but you were not there. I saw the car parked so I imagined you had not gone far and I know this path is really pleasant…" He stopped, and looking at her, all his doubts faded.

"Maria, can we sit down for a moment?" He pointed at a bench but she thought she preferred the intimacy of her home.

"Jason, you didn't drink that coffee last Monday. What about coming to me for a good Italian coffee now?" she smiled and wondered if he would refuse, considering his behaviour in the last few days, but he simply replied, "I think it's a good idea, Maria."

The walk back to her home seemed interminable to both of them, they were both thinking what to say next and they were both absorbed in their feelings.

Maria opened the door to her bungalow and let Jason in. She went silently to the living room and she invited Jason to sit on the sofa. She sat on the armchair next to it. She was so agitated she completely forgot the coffee.

Jason sat on the edge of the sofa and looked at her for some moments.

"Maria, what I am going to tell you is something only Father Mark knows. Maria, I am really ashamed of my behaviour in the last few days." Maria looked at him and waited. "In reality, I behaved like a fool because I realized when I came to you last Monday that… that you are a wonderful woman, you are sensitive, considerate, reserved… I… I… I am growing fond of you, Maria!"

Maria was afraid she would faint because she realized she had been waiting for these words. It seemed as if the world had suddenly stood still, there was no Canada, Italy, Trinity, Padua, just the two of them. She couldn't talk, she just waited for him to go on. She felt that what he would say next was costing him very much. She didn't want to press him or make him more nervous. She knew he would speak when he felt like it.

"Maria, when I discovered, when I felt I was growing… falling in love with you I was afraid. Six years ago something terrible happened to me, you see that it is difficult for me to talk about it even now."

He lowered his gaze for a few moments and Maria instinctively sat down beside him on the sofa and took his hands. She wanted to make him feel that she was there for him, that she would comfort him.

He looked straight ahead and started to speak almost mechanically, as if he was trying to detach himself from what he was saying.

"When I was seventeen my mother and father told me that I would have a little sister. I was so happy," he smiled as he recalled those joyful moments. "My sister Anna was seven and I was twenty-four, I had just become a policeman when my parents both died in a car accident." Maria blinked back the tears that were coming to her eyes.

"I was left with a little sister, and at first, I thought that it would be a problem, I had a job, friends, a girlfriend. Father Mark always helped me during that period. Instead, Anna was the greatest joy of my life. She was a sweet child and then a sensitive teenager, she adored me and I adored her." 'That's why he is so kind to teenage girls,' Maria thought. "It was wonderful to see her grow up. We were really happy, she prepared breakfast for me on Sundays, we went to baseball games together and she liked playing volleyball! She always understood when I was worried and sad and I always saw when she had something on her mind. I often told Mark that she was a gift that my parents had left me. We lived in Toronto then and Father Mark directed the school where both Anna and I studied."

He turned and looked at Maria. He was amazed at how easily words came to him now.

"Yes, Maria, Anna is the pretty girl in the photo on my desk! Here in Trinity, only my colleagues at the police station know what happened. I saw Hogan watch the picture on my desk once or twice but he has never dared to ask me or to say anything, even if I know he sympathizes with me."

Now came the part that was more difficult for Jason and Maria imagined a tragedy had happened.

"When she was twenty, I took part in a raid to arrest a serial killer who had murdered several women. There was a shooting and I saw he was going to kill one of my agents, so I shot and killed him." He bent his head and stopped. Maria caressed his hand that was still in hers. He turned and said sadly, "Don't think that being a policeman, I am used to killing people. It is something hard to accept for me even now, even when the victim is a serial killer who has murdered innocent women and even children."

Maria instinctively caressed Jason's face and she waited patiently for the worst part that, she knew, was yet to come.

Jason sighed deeply and went on, "That serial killer had a brother, a gangster we have not been able to arrest yet. He is a very cunning man, he has connections and a lot of people who cover him. One day, I went home after work and…" this was really too much even for a tough man like Jason. He had to stop and he started sobbing. Maria told him,

"I imagine the rest, Jason. I am so sorry!" Tears were coming down her cheeks too.

"I found my sister in a pool of blood on the porch of my home and a message written on a piece of paper, 'Now we are even!'" Maria couldn't restrain herself any longer and she embraced him. They remained like that for minutes, they were both crying but Jason was feeling a strange sense of relief because he had finally been able to tell someone what had happened.

After a time, time meant nothing for them now, Jason gently freed himself from Maria's embrace.

He looked at her with tearful eyes and kindly wiped her tears from her face.

"I am sorry, Maria," he tried to smile and said, "This is not what is usually meant for a first date!" He sat back on the sofa and continued to talk, always holding Maria's hand, "That gangster had an alibi and we were not able to pin my sister's murder on him, even if I am sure he was responsible or behind Anna's death. At that period, I had had a girlfriend for some time; she got on well with my sister and I thought it was something serious, but after the death of Anna she moved away from me little by little. I couldn't and I cannot blame her, I was really devastated and I imagine it was difficult to stand beside me. I let her go and from that moment I promised myself never to have relationships in my life because I am afraid I could put the people I love in danger. This is why I instinctively avoided you." Now he looked at her with a troubled face, "Furthermore, Maria, we have not been able to catch that bastard yet. Excuse me, but I cannot find another way to define him. I will never be at rest until I have arrested him!"

Maria looked at him sadly and replied, "Jason, I am so sorry for your sister. You must have been a wonderful brother." Oh, how she wished she had had a sister like that; caring and affectionate. "But if that gangster said, 'Now we are even!' maybe he means he has completed his revenge, or whatever that shameful murder is for him, maybe he will not try to hurt you or your dear ones any more."

Jason shook his head and reflected for a few moments before answering, "Maybe you are right, but my job is dangerous and can put the lives of the people around me in danger anyway. I still have the feeling that my sister would still be alive if I hadn't been a policeman. The fact is that I deal with the worst unscrupulous criminals, being the head of the Homicide Department. What am I to do, Maria? I don't want to put your life in danger but I can't live without seeing you and the more I tried to tell myself that I had to keep to myself, the more I wanted to come here and talk to you. You understand my trouble, don't you?"

Maria nodded but now she was smiling and she said, "Jason, you can't stay isolated from the world. You can't deny your feelings and you mustn't blame yourself for what happened to your sister. It is not your fault!" She understood that now she had to talk about herself and she said, trying to keep her voice steady but betraying the emotion that almost prevented her from talking, "Jason, I arrived a month ago from Italy and I don't even know if I will be confirmed in my job next year." Jason smiled but didn't say what Father Mark had told him. "But you are a wonderful man. I saw you with Meg that day, you are sensitive, professional and I know you have a big heart, you care for the people and you took care of a little sister…" she had to stop because her emotions were overwhelming her. "Jason, I want to get to know you better, I am really fond of you. I am feeling for you what I have never felt for any other man in my life. Jason, please, I don't care if my life will be in danger, don't give up on me, please! If there will be danger you will protect me, but give us a chance... Please!" she stopped and he looked at her with infinite tenderness. Now he could not back out, he could not keep her at a distance, now only Mark's prayers could help them and preserve them from danger. As if Maria had read his thoughts, she added, "And Jason, remember that we are religious and that I firmly believe that the Divine Providence will always help us if what we feel for each other is true!"

Jason said with force, "It is true, Maria!" he leaned towards her and he gently kissed her lips. Then he embraced her tenderly and they remained lost in that embrace for... a few minutes? A quarter of an hour? Time meant nothing, there were only Jason and Maria and their love.

After a time of tenderness, Jason turned to her and said, "But you haven't said anything about you, about your family. You were so sad last Monday and I don't know anything about your life, apart from the fact that you are a wonderful teacher." He saw the troubled expression on Maria's face and he stopped, "Maria, I have already saddened you enough today. If you don't want to talk about it, if it is something that makes you suffer..." his voice trailed off because Maria had gone to retrieve her bag. She went back to sit on the sofa next to him. She took out her father's letter, knowing that Jason couldn't read it because it was written in Italian, but she thought that it would help her to explain. She clutched the wedding ring and Jason said, "I have noticed you often touch that wedding ring, Maria," he was thinking maybe she was a widow.

Maria raised her eyes and looked at him with love, "Jason, if you have found the courage to tell me what weighed on your heart, I will do the same. In fact, I am ashamed because I have not experienced a terrible tragedy like you. This ring," she held it between her fingers and showed it to Jason, "belonged to my dad, or I should say to my stepfather."

As it had been relatively easy for Jason to speak about his past, it was now for Maria much less difficult than she had expected to explain the content of the letter and to talk about her stepmother and stepsister, considering that, since her dad's death, Maria had spoken to nobody about the letter, not to her colleagues or her friends in the parish. While she was talking, she had to stop a few times, overwhelmed by the emotion, and Jason kept on caressing her face, her hands and he looked at her with infinite tenderness. He didn't say, as many people around her had done, that it was not possible, that her stepmother had certainly loved her. When she had finished she was crying with the emotion, for the longing for her dad to be there with her, for the bitterness that always pervaded her soul when she talked about Raffaella and her wickedness. Jason cradled her in his arms, waiting for her to calm down, without saying a word, but she felt he had understood, he was really sympathizing with her suffering for many years because of the lack of a real family, he was really sharing her pain with her as she had shared his desperation for a sister who had died so young, in such a cruel way.

Now that they had confessed what was in the bottoms of their hearts, they realized it was well past the evening mass Maria had intended to attend. Maria offered to prepare dinner and Jason accepted. The rest of the evening was spent serenely in the joy of being together. They talked about their job, about Italy, about the plans for the following weekends. Maria showed Jason pictures of her dad and her hometown and they discovered that very evening that they enjoyed each other's company, that they delighted in talking and in feeling the warmth of each other's presence. This was really for Maria and Jason, A NEW BEGINNING!

Epilogue

Sunday, October 12th

Mark was preparing to celebrate the morning mass on the day before Thanksgiving, but this mass was really a Thanksgiving celebration because Andy and Grace Cooper would renew their wedding vows after twenty years of marriage and after so much suffering and worry only a few weeks before.

As he came out of the sacristy and climbed the three steps that led to the altar, he turned to face the crowded church in front of him and his heart was really joyful and grateful to the Creator who had given him so much grace in his years of priesthood.

He thanked God for Andy and Grace, who were sitting in the front pew with their daughter, Meg, and their relatives. They were elegant and smiling, a really beautiful family united in love and respect, living an honest and serene life and bringing up their daughter in the values of faith, generosity and righteousness. They had faced the time of danger, prison and of false accusations, united in their mutual love and now they were enjoying the affection of many people gathered in the church to pray with them and for them.

He thanked God for Louise, who was sitting between her uncle and aunt, with a radiant and happy countenance, so different from the worried look she had only a few weeks before between her father and mother. Yes, it would not be easy for her, because all the love of her aunt and uncle could not substitute for the suffering her parents had caused her, but she was not alone, she had someone to support her and give her all the affection she had longed for, for more than sixteen years.

He thanked God for Miss Lewis, who was in church today, invited by the Coopers. She had completely recovered and she was serene. Mark hoped she would start to participate in the community, so that she would be a little less lonely, but he knew that for her now the most important thing was having her job and being able to take care of her sick mother....

He thanked God for Agent Hogan and his wife, Sue, invited by the Coopers. They had had their share of worries and suffering but now Sue was better and Mark prayed her periodical check-ups would confirm the remission from cancer.

But his heart was really full of joy and gratitude for Jason and Maria. They were sitting next to each other behind

Louise and her relatives. Father Mark had prayed so much that Jason could find comfort in his loss. As they looked at each other at the beginning of the mass, Mark saw love, admiration, mutual support and understanding and he said really and from the heart,

'Thank God, because in your mysterious design you never leave us alone. Protect them, please! They have already suffered so much!' A week before they had gone to him to tell him the good news and they had tears in their eyes for the emotion of that moment. He had taken them to church and together they had thanked the Lord and prayed to Him to protect them.

He thanked God for all the students, schoolmates of Meg and Louise, and all the teachers he saw in church with their families. Without them, his life would be empty, he filled it with their stories, their personal lives, their joys and their sorrows...

He thanked God for Angela Dawson and her husband, Tony. Angela was the only one in church who seemed detached and troubled. Tony had come to him a few days before and he had asked him to pray for his wife because he had told him that she had to deal with something from the past that tormented her. Mark sighed. He would concentrate his prayers on her as he had seen she was restless and anxious but he knew that, when she felt like it, she would come to him, as everybody did.

But for her, as for most of the people in front of Him, this was really A NEW BEGINNING!

'Monday, October 13th

Dear Giulio,

I couldn't miss my Monday appointment with you. Thanks for your words of encouragement and your prayers for me and Jason. Have you seen the photos? Isn't he handsome? I know, I have already told you that I feel like a teenager with her first love, but Giulio, I am so happy I think my heart could explode.

You know that I had some boyfriends in the past, with one or two I thought I could start something really serious, but I think that my dad told you, as he often told me, that he would understand that I had found the real, the true one when he saw a different light in my eyes. Now there is a different light in my eyes, can you see that in the photos?

Today is Thanksgiving day here in Canada and there is no school. I have just returned with Jason from Niagara Falls.

Yesterday, we had a big celebration because Andy and Grace Cooper, the parents of one of my best students, Meg, renewed their wedding vows after twenty years. Andy was the one who went to prison for that murder I talked to you about, but luckily, he was released after Jason arrested the real murderer and now they are the happy family they have always been.

After the mass and the refreshments, Jason and I left with one of his agents, David Hogan, and his wife, who have a small cottage not far from Niagara Falls. Sue Hogan is recovering after therapy against cancer, but she is better and they invited us to spend Thanksgiving with them. They are really nice and we had a wonderful evening yesterday. I made Tiramisu and they all liked it.

This morning, I went with Jason to see the falls, they are really spectacular and breathtaking. We took a boat that brought us as far as it was safe near the falls. I was a little scared because they were really imposing. The colours of Autumn are incredible. I enclose a lot of photos, I hope you like them.

We had lunch at a restaurant overlooking the falls and then we drove back home.

Now Jason has had to go to the police station to catch up with his papers and I am correcting my students' homework.

When I went with Jason last week to Father Mark to tell him that we had decided to be a couple or at least to try to get to know each other better, he didn't say it clearly, but he hinted at the fact that he will confirm me as a teacher next year.

I hope so, but now I know that my place is next to Jason and that, Italian teacher or not, I will remain here.

Are you really thinking of coming to Canada? It would be wonderful! Please say you will. Father Mark and Jason send you their love. Pray for me, Giulio, I am asking the Lord and the Virgin Mary to teach me to be able to stand beside Jason in every moment, to be able to give him the support he needs and to be grateful for the love and tenderness he is bestowing on me every day. I am so lucky.

This is MY NEW BEGINNING.

Love,

Yours truly, happy Maria'

OUT OF DANGER
Miracle High School Mysteries
Second Book

Teaser

A man was watching the happy couple from afar. He was sitting on a bench in the little harbour and he had a newspaper in his hands that he was ready to raise in front of him in case Jason looked his way. He was a bad man, who had killed several people already, especially women and he had always been able to avoid arrest. He had a particular liking for brunettes or women with dark, blond hair.

He was a man in his early forties, the younger of two brothers. He had receding, dark hair and a thin beard, with a long, oval face and small evil, eyes and was short and muscular. His older brother had been killed by that policeman, Grant. Luckily for him, his brother was completely different from him; tall and stocky, brown-haired and with a round face. He hated that policeman, he would have liked to kill him too, but it was too risky. When he had murdered Grant's sister, the street was deserted but then some neighbours arrived and he had to hide quickly. Then he disappeared for some time and he promised his 'friends', who had given him a watertight alibi for that and other murders, that he would remain 'clean', but when he saw a woman with beautiful brown or blond hair, a pretty figure and a sweet smile, he couldn't resist. Why didn't those women he approached want anything to do with him? Why had all the women he had met refused him? Tonight, he was very nervous because Grant's woman attracted him. Oh, she had such soft hair, such a charming smile and such a beautiful body. And why did women want to stay with that Detective he hated so much? What did Grant have that he didn't? Now there were too many people around but he decided to follow her more closely. He had to be careful, very careful, because sometimes he got reckless and lost control, and once or twice, the police had been too close to arresting him. He had to be careful. Maybe he had better follow the advice of his friends and remain as clean as he could, but... he couldn't resist the charm of a woman. Maybe if he talked to her about Grant, she would change her mind about him, and if not,... another occasion for revenge.

He realized he was becoming more and more nervous so he got up from the bench and went home, but one of the following days, he promised himself...